ALL NIGHT WITH DARCY

A PRIDE AND PREJUDICE VARIATION

JANE GRIX

Cover design by beetifulbookcovers.com
Cover image by olly/stock.adobe.com

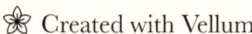 Created with Vellum

PROLOGUE

THE LONGBOURN PARTY was the last of all the company to leave Netherfield after the ball. Fitzwilliam Darcy stood off to one side, not wanting to engage in conversation as the Bennets waited for their carriage to arrive. He purposefully avoided looking directly at Miss Elizabeth Bennet.

His friend Charles Bingley, as host for the evening's activities, spoke politely to Mrs. Bennet. Better you than I, Darcy thought. He found Mrs. Bennet unbearable. She was a vulgar, silly woman who wanted nothing more than to see her five daughters advantageously married. As a gentleman with a fortune of more than ten thousand pounds a year and a beautiful estate in Derbyshire, Darcy had met her kind numerous times in London, but Mrs.

Bennet was particularly obnoxious. She was currently promoting her eldest daughter Jane to Bingley.

Jane Bennet was an attractive, sweet-natured girl of above average intelligence, but Darcy thought Bingley could do much better. From what Darcy could tell, Jane was a dutiful daughter who only encouraged Bingley's attentions because of her mother. She had a calm, serene countenance that implied that her heart was not affected by him at all. Darcy hoped, for the sake of Bingley's future happiness, that he would find a young woman who would love him sincerely for his good qualities and not just for his fortune.

Bingley's sisters, a Miss Bingley and Mrs. Hurst, were fashionable, insincere women who lived for their own comforts and entertained themselves with shopping, cards, and gossip. They had enjoyed the noise and spectacle of the evening's activities, but now they were impatient to have the house to themselves. They scarcely opened their mouths except to complain of fatigue. Darcy watched as one of the blue ostrich feathers on Miss Bingley's orange headdress drooped low over one of her eyes. She, noticing his gaze and mistaking it for admiration, smirked with satisfaction and he looked away, not wanting to encourage her.

Mr. Collins, a cousin of the Bennets, droned on, complimenting Mr. Bingley and his sisters on the elegance of their entertainment and the hospitality and politeness which had marked their behaviour to their guests.

What a fool, Darcy thought, but he kept his face expressionless so as not to reveal his annoyance. Mr. Collins was a clergyman and Darcy was glad that he did not have to hear his sermons, although he supposed he would have to hear one or two when he visited his aunt Lady Catherine de Bourgh at Easter. Mr. Collins was her vicar, which was additional reason to dread going to visit his aunt. Darcy did not enjoy his annual trips to visit his aunt in Kent because she wanted him to marry her daughter Anne, and as both he and Anne advanced in years, Lady Catherine's attempts to force a union between them became more marked.

Darcy felt a twinge of pity for Anne. Her health was not good and she rarely went anywhere. She was like a prisoner of Rosings Park with Lady Catherine as her jailor.

Although Darcy often missed his parents who had died years earlier, he appreciated the fact that he could now do what he wished and go where he wished without having to please anyone.

And in the morning, he would leave for London and put this provincial town behind him.

Against his better judgment, Darcy glanced briefly at the young woman who had inspired his current desire to flee the county - Elizabeth Bennet.

She, like he, was silent as her irritating cousin and vulgar mother chattered on.

Elizabeth Bennet wore a lovely white gown with gold ribbons. Her dark hair was arranged in curls with one ringlet that fell across a creamy shoulder. She was a pretty girl, no beauty like her sister Jane, but it wasn't merely her physical attributes that had upset his equilibrium.

No, it was something more astonishing. When they first met, the month before, he had slighted her at a local Assembly and she had laughed at him.

Her laugh changed him.

Unlike the hundreds of women who had flattered him since he had reached his majority, Elizabeth was her own woman – independent and clever.

He had found himself intrigued, then fascinated, and now, only a few weeks later, he believed that he was falling in love with her.

This would never do.

He had danced with her tonight and for a few moments, with her hand in his, with his hand at her waist, he had been tempted to take her out into the moonlit gardens, kiss her and propose to her.

It was madness.

The surge of emotion he felt had horrified him and he was now determined to put her behind him.

He knew she was completely unsuitable to be Mistress of Pemberley, his family estate. His friends and extended family would be appalled if they met her vulgar family and connections. Elizabeth had an uncle who was a lawyer and another engaged in Trade. Her father, although a gentleman by birth, had done little to curb the excesses of his family.

The youngest Bennet, he did not know if it was Lydia or her sister who was called Kitty, yawned, forgetting to cover her mouth with a gloved hand, and exclaimed, "Lord, how tired I am."

Darcy set his jaw in a firm line. Remember this, he told himself. If you marry Elizabeth, you will be brother to her sisters.

But she would be your wife, his traitorous thoughts continued. Darcy imagined the thrill of waking next to Elizabeth, knowing that she was his completely.

Mrs. Bennet's shrill voice interrupted his

musings. Mrs. Bennet told Bingley how happy he would make her if he would eat a family dinner with them. "You can come at any time, without the ceremony of a formal invitation. Even tomorrow night, or I suppose I should say tonight since it is early in the morning." She giggled at her own attempt at humour.

Bingley did seem a little surprised by her exuberance, but he said graciously, "I would be happy to come any evening, but first I must go to London. I am leaving tomorrow."

"Oh no," Mrs. Bennet cried. "I hope your visit will not be a long one, for we would miss your terribly."

"It is only for a few days."

"Excellent," Mrs. Bennet said. "And we shall count on your joining us for dinner as soon as you return."

Darcy saw a look of embarrassment pass across Elizabeth's face. She glanced at him briefly with her beautiful dark eyes as if wanting to see his reaction.

Darcy clenched his teeth and glanced down at the gloves in his hands.

Fortunately for Darcy's peace of mind, the Bennet's transportation finally arrived and a footman helped the Bennets into their carriage.

Bingley wished them all a safe journey.

Darcy took one last look at Elizabeth and turned away. He knew his duty. He knew what was owed to his name and station.

It would be best if he never saw her again.

CHAPTER ONE

FIVE MONTHS LATER

Darcy sat at a square table in one of the drawing rooms at Rosings Park, playing cards with his aunt, Lady Catherine, his cousin Anne and another cousin, Colonel Fitzwilliam. Lady Catherine was discussing plans for the following evening and said that they would have additional company for dinner – Mr. Collins and his new wife, as well as their guests, Mrs. Collin's younger sister and a Miss Bennet.

Darcy flinched. For a moment, he felt as if a dagger had been thrust into his heart. He had tried not to think of Elizabeth Bennet for months and now she was practically on his aunt's doorstep? He forced his voice to remain calm. "Which Miss Bennet?" he asked, hoping that it was her eldest sister Jane who was staying with the Collinses.

"Her name is Elizabeth," Lady Catherine provided. "Are you acquainted with her?"

"A little," he said carefully. "Her family are neighbours to one of my good friends."

"Which friend?"

"Mr. Bingley."

"Ah. Bingley." Lady Catherine sniffed her disapproval. She knew that Mr. Bingley's fortune had been made in Trade two generations back and she thought him a poor companion to her nephew. She thought he should spend more time with her nephews who were sons of her brother, an earl.

Darcy said, "Yes. Mr. Bingley recently rented a home in Hertfordshire and I visited there several weeks in the autumn."

Anne asked quietly, "Was your visit pleasant?"

Anne's voice was so soft that her mother often spoke over her, not hearing her, but Darcy turned to her and said, "Primarily, yes."

"I should like to see Hertfordshire someday," Anne added.

Lady Catherine said firmly, "You know we are

going to Bath later this summer. That will be ample travelling for the year."

"Yes, Mama," Anne said calmly and looked down at the cards in her hands.

Poor Anne, Darcy thought. Lady Catherine had taken Anne to drink the waters in Bath for years with little improvement.

"Is Miss Bennet a pretty girl?" Colonel Fitzwilliam asked.

Lady Catherine frowned, her dark eyebrows furrowing. "She is not for you, Fitzwilliam," she answered sharply.

"No dowry?" the Colonel guessed. The Colonel was the third son of the Earl of Matlock and had expensive tastes. He would need to marry an heiress.

"Not enough to speak of," Lady Catherine said dismissively. "It is not more than a thousand pounds. It would have been enough for Mr. Collins, but not enough for you."

"Mr. Collins?" Darcy asked. "Did he want to marry Miss Bennet?"

"Yes. He is her cousin and last year, when he went to visit the family, he went with the plan of marrying one of the daughters. But Miss Elizabeth refused him, and he married a neighbour, Miss

Lucas instead, which surprised me. However, having met both women now I thoroughly approve of his choice. Miss Elizabeth Bennet expresses her opinions much too decidedly."

Which was one of the things Darcy had liked best about her, although he would not admit it out loud.

"Which would make her a most uncomfortable wife, even if she did have a larger dowry," Lady Catherine continued.

Darcy glanced at the Colonel and saw the amusement in his eyes. Both of them found Lady Catherine's comments ironic, for her criticism of Elizabeth Bennet was a case of the pot calling the kettle black. From what they had observed, Lady Catherine had been a most uncomfortable wife as well. Her husband Sir Lewis had been a quiet, timid man, who spent his days improving Rosings' library and its extensive wine cellar. When in company with his wife, he had said little, for she had spoken more than enough for both of them.

Anne, who seemed to have more of her father's temperament said quietly, "Miss Bennet can play the pianoforte."

"Excellent," the Colonel said. "I look forward to some music."

"I am taking lessons as well," Anne volunteered meekly.

Darcy was surprised. This was a new development. In the past, Lady Catherine had said that Anne did not have the physical strength to play a musical instrument.

"Would you like to play for us?" Darcy asked. It would make a pleasant change from playing cards.

"Oh no," Anne said. Her face flamed red with embarrassment. "I am not ready to perform in public. Not yet."

Lady Catherine waved her fears away. "Nonsense. You are better than you think," she said and turned to Darcy. "She has just started her lessons, but I am certain that in a few months, she will surpass even Miss Bennet's skill, for she has a most expensive tutor that I hired from London. One of our neighbours in Bath, Lady Hodge recommended him. A Signor Bianchi. Have you heard of him?"

The name sounded familiar to Darcy and he wondered if there had been some gossip about him. "Is he Italian?"

"Yes, but his English is excellent. He has hardly any accent."

As if that mattered, Darcy thought.

That evening, as he and the Colonel walked

upstairs to retire, Darcy mentioned that he wished to pay a morning visit to the Parsonage. "I am acquainted with both Mrs. Collins and Miss Bennet. It is the civil thing to do."

The Colonel was surprised. "Agreed," he said pleasantly. "Heaven knows the exercise will do us both good, but when have you ever cared about civility?'

ELIZABETH BENNET SAT in the Parsonage sitting room next to her dear friend Charlotte, Mrs. Collins now, as they both hemmed shirts for Mr. Collins.

Elizabeth worked steadily. She was a mediocre needlewoman, but hemming was a peaceful, simple task that gave her opportunity for reflection.

She had debated on the wisdom of coming to Hunsford for weeks. On one hand, she wanted to see her friend again, but on the other, she did not want to spend time with Charlotte's new husband – Mr. Collins, the man she had rejected only five months before.

She remembered their uncomfortable conversation. In his pedantic way, Mr. Collins had begun by outlining his many reasons for marriage, then assured her of the violence of his affection and ended by promising not to reproach her for her small dowry.

His proposal had been ridiculous, offensive, and amusing, and then alarming when he refused to believe her refusal. She had begun her rejection with politeness but then had to be quite stern to convince him that she would never marry him.

Mr. Collins had not mourned his loss for long, for he had proposed to Charlotte two days later and professed to love her even more than he had professed to love Elizabeth. Elizabeth was not insulted by his fickleness, but she wondered at her friend's wisdom in accepting such a silly, annoying man. But Charlotte had wanted security, and now, seeing how comfortably she was settled in the Parsonage with her private sitting room, her garden and her servants, Elizabeth was reconciled to the union.

As Jane often said, there was no accounting for taste, and it should not matter if they did not like Mr. Collins as long as Charlotte did.

In theory, Elizabeth agreed, but she knew that she could never have been happy with such an arrangement. Not only was Mr. Collins intolerable, but his neighbour and patroness Lady Catherine de Bourgh was an overbearing domestic tyrant. She felt free to control all of Charlotte's household. Lady Catherine was a tall, imposing woman with a stern air, which reminded Elizabeth of her nephew Mr. Darcy.

Mr. Darcy, Elizabeth thought with a frown as she took another stitch. Charlotte had said that he and his cousin, a Colonel Fitzwilliam, would be visiting Lady Catherine any day now.

"Do you think we will see them?" Elizabeth had asked.

"I don't think so," Charlotte had said. "Or if we do, it will only be briefly. Lady Catherine does not usually invite us for tea or to dine when she has company."

Elizabeth stabbed her needle into the white fabric. She would be perfectly happy never to see Mr. Darcy again.

Elizabeth had met Mr. Darcy in October the year before, when he visited his friend Bingley in Hertfordshire. Initially Elizabeth had found him to be a tall, handsome man, and she had eagerly anticipated getting to know him better until his appalling manners and superior attitude had changed her mind.

She had overheard him telling Mr. Bingley at a local Assembly that she was not handsome enough to dance with.

It was so absurd a complaint that she had laughed out loud. Infuriating man.

Mr. Darcy might be handsome, but in her opinion, handsome was as handsome did, and she would prefer a hideous man with a good heart over a handsome man with his mean one.

And Mr. Darcy did have a cold, hard heart. Not only did he think himself superior to everyone in Meryton and look down on her with disdain, Mr. Darcy had ruined the prospects of one of Elizabeth's new friends, a Mr. Wickham.

Poor Mr. Wickham, Elizabeth thought with a sigh.

He was the most charming man of her acquaintance. He was handsome, tall, although a few inches short of Mr. Darcy's massive frame, and he was blessed with easy, open manners.

He was a soldier, currently stationed outside Meryton, only a few miles from her home. For a few weeks in the autumn, he had singled her out for his attentions, so much so that her aunt Mrs. Gardiner had warned her not to fall in love with him. "It would not be prudent," she said. What she meant was that Wickham did not have the means to support a family, and Elizabeth knew she was correct.

Mr. Wickham had told Elizabeth of his misfortunes, how Mr. Darcy had refused to honour a bequest in his father's will. Mr. Darcy Senior, Mr. Wickham's godfather, had intended Mr. Wickham to become a clergyman and offered him a living in his will, but when the opening came available, the younger Mr. Darcy refused to give it.

Mr. Wickham had been forced to find other employment, so he had joined the army. And then, more recently, he had become engaged to a local heiress Miss King who had an inheritance of ten thousand pounds.

Elizabeth did not blame him. She knew that handsome men must have something to live on, as well as plain ones.

But it did seem unfair to her for Mr. Darcy who had been blessed with an abundance to be so cruel. She had asked Mr. Wickham why he had done it – how Mr. Darcy could deny a man who had been his childhood companion. For he and Wickham had grown up together. Mr. Wickham's father had been the Senior Mr. Darcy's steward.

Mr. Wickham had explained, "Mr. Darcy has

always been jealous of me, of my closeness to his father. Mr. Darcy is a man who cannot bear any sort of competition unless he knows he will win."

"Shameful!"

"What is that?" Charlotte asked, and Elizabeth realized she must have spoken out loud. "My stitches," she said with a smile. "I have pulled the thread too tight and will have to redo the past few inches."

She and Charlotte worked in silence for the next few minutes, and then to Elizabeth's horror, Mr. Darcy and his cousin appeared on the doorstep, accompanied by Mr. Collins. "My dear, look whom I have found!" Mr. Collins exclaimed as he brought the gentlemen into the house. "Mr. Darcy and Colonel Fitzwilliam. Just consider the felicity of the moment. I was on my way to meet them, just as they were on their way to meet me!"

Mr. Darcy was just as Elizabeth remembered. Tall and stern.

Introductions were made and Mr. Darcy made his compliments to Mrs. Collins on her recent marriage, then fell silent and scowled at her.

Odious man.

Elizabeth turned her attentions to Colonel Fitzwilliam. He was about thirty, not handsome, but in person and address, most truly the gentleman.

He spoke easily with the confidence of a well-bred man. Mr. Darcy should take lessons from his cousin, Elizabeth thought with a smile.

After a few minutes, Mr. Darcy interrupted her conversation with the Colonel to enquire after the health of her family.

Elizabeth startled. "Are you speaking to me, Mr. Darcy?"

"Yes."

"Oh. I thought you meant to be silent today and merely observe rather than participate in the conversation."

The Colonel choked back a laugh. "She has you to rights, Darcy. You are like a statue today."

Mr. Darcy stiffened. "Like you, Miss Bennet, I enjoy studying the behaviour of others, but I hope that I am capable of speaking when necessary."

"Do you only speak out of duty, Mr. Darcy?" Elizabeth asked.

Mr. Collins' eyes grew wide at her impertinence and his mouth dropped open as he tried to think of something conciliatory to say.

Mr. Darcy smiled. "I know you are teasing me, but I do not mind it. And yes, Miss Bennet, sometimes I do speak out of duty, when I would prefer silence. Society makes demands upon us all, but surely it is better to err on the side of discretion than to speak too much."

"Excellent observation," Mr. Collins said, nodding his approval. "Too many people say too much, not thinking about what they are disclosing and how they might expose themselves to ridicule. As the Proverb states, 'whoso keepeth his mouth and his tongue keepeth his soul from troubles.'"

"I believe we have all said things we regret," Elizabeth agreed. Today she regretted needling Mr. Darcy with her wit, for now he stood near her, as if wanting to converse more privately with her.

But fortunately, Mr. Collins had found a new topic that he refused to abandon. He continued with his impromptu sermon. "I have often discussed this passage with Lady Catherine. As the Bible states, 'Let no corrupt communication proceed out of your mouth, but that which is good to the use of edifying, that it may minister gracc unto the hearers.' Not that you would ever speak corruption, Mr. Darcy, and I have often noticed that everything you say is edifying. In that respect, I believe you follow your aunt's superior example."

Mr. Darcy schooled his face into bland acceptance. "Sir," he said with a nod.

Elizabeth bit her lip and had to look down at her needlework to keep from laughing.

Mr. Collins spoke longer but eventually he tired.

When the conversation lagged, and Mr. Darcy continued to watch her closely, Elizabeth took the opportunity to speak to him. She said, "My eldest sister has been in town these three months. Have you never happened to see her there?"

For a moment, Mr. Darcy looked a little confused as if he would say one thing and then changed his mind. He said stiffly, "I have never been so fortunate as to meet Miss Bennet."

His response was so oddly worded, Elizabeth wondered if he were hiding something from her.

Then shortly after this, the gentlemen took their leave. Charlotte suggested to her husband that he go to his study and record some of his thoughts for a new sermon.

"You are right, my dear," he said. "I should record my thoughts while they are fresh before me." He turned to Elizabeth. "You see, dear Cousin, how your friend is a helpmeet to me. I could not be happier with my choice of companions." He caught himself and added quickly, "But perhaps the less said on this matter, the better. Only let me assure you, that I can from my heart most cordially wish you equal felicity in marriage. My dear Charlotte and I have but one mind and one way of thinking. There is in every thing a most remarkable resemblance of character and ideas between us. We seem to have been designed for each other."

Elizabeth chose her words carefully. She smiled and said, "It is a great happiness when that is the case."

Charlotte cleared her throat. "Mr. Collins, your study?" she prompted and that large man, after a few additional verbose praises for her kind suggestion, wandered down the hall.

Elizabeth waited until the door had closed before she breathed out a long sigh. "Oh, Charlotte." She thought, "how can you bear being married to that man?" but out of kindness, she did not say it.

Charlotte smiled. "I know what you are thinking, Elizabeth, but you are mistaken if you think I am unhappy. Mr. Collins is a good man, perhaps not as sensible as your Mr. Darcy, but no worse than my father."

Elizabeth sputtered. "My Mr. Darcy? Whatever can you mean?"

Charlotte said, "Yes. I believe he will be yours,

if you will have him. The way he stares at you is so romantic."

"Romantic?" Elizabeth argued. "He thoroughly dislikes me."

"Not from what I observe. Remember you were the only woman he danced with at the Netherfield Ball. And you should have seen the way he glared at the Colonel when you talked and smiled at him today. No, I think Mr. Darcy likes you very much. And I know we owe your presence for this morning visit. Mr. Darcy would never have come so soon to wait on only me."

Elizabeth shook her head. "I think marriage has addled your brain, Charlotte."

CHAPTER TWO

DARCY THOUGHT of Elizabeth for several days, but through sheer strength of will, he forced himself to keep away from the Parsonage.

He kept himself busy by riding, playing billiards with Colonel Fitzwilliam and reading. One day while walking about Rosings, Darcy came upon Signor Bianchi sitting beside Anne at the pianoforte, teaching his lesson. At Darcy's entrance to the music room, both of them startled. Signor Bianchi scrambled to his feet. Signor Bianchi was a handsome man in his early forties. "Forgive me," Darcy said. "Would you like me to leave?"

"Oh no, Signor." There was something in Signor Bianchi's tone of voice that bothered Darcy. It was not his accent, it was his smug tone, as if he were amused by something that he knew and Darcy did not.

Darcy decided that he did not like him – not his swarthy good looks, his muscular shoulders, or his long curly dark hair that was tied at his neck with a black ribbon.

"Please sit down," the instructor continued with a wave of his hand. "and let Miss de Bourgh enchant you."

Anne blushed at the praise and proceeded to play a short piece, full of errors.

Excruciating, Darcy thought, but he supposed that a beginner would make errors.

"Bellissimo," Signor Bianchi said. "Every day you improve, Miss de Bourgh."

If Signor Bianchi were Irish, Darcy would think he had kissed the Blarney Stone.

"What did you think?" Anne asked.

Darcy lied. "Very nice." He looked about the room. "But where is Mrs. Jenkinson?"

Anne blushed guiltily. "She stepped outside to fetch a shawl for me."

And true to her word, in a moment, Mrs. Jenkinson returned to the room with a shawl in hand. She carefully draped it around Anne's shoulders and then sat down several feet away from the pianoforte to chaperone the lesson.

Propriety was restored, but Darcy was not satisfied.

He sought out his cousin in the library. "Richard," he said abruptly. "Have you met Signor Bianchi?"

The Colonel set aside the volume he was reading. "I may have seen him in the hallways once or twice. Medium height. Dark?"

"Yes."

The Colonel said, "What is the problem?"

Darcy said, "I don't know if there is a problem. But I think he may try to take advantage of Anne."

The Colonel laughed. "Anne? He's not blind, is he?"

Darcy thought that was unkind. It wasn't Anne's fault that her health was poor. She was thin and sallow and pain had left a permanent furrow over her brow. "Remember that she is the heir to Rosings."

"But what fortune hunter is going to get past Lady Catherine?"

Darcy said, "Perhaps you are right and I am worrying about nothing. But I think he is flirting with her."

"Doesn't every instructor flirt with his female students? I remember my two younger sisters and my mother swooning over a dance instructor last year, but there was no harm done."

"The Countess?" Darcy said, trying to imagine his august aunt swooning. "Truly?"

The Colonel laughed. "Yes. I heard her giggle during a waltz."

Amazing. Darcy said, "I seem to remember some kind of gossip about Signor Bianchi, but I can't remember the particulars."

"Aunt Catherine's friend would not have recommended him if he were a complete scoundrel."

Darcy was not so sure of that. Wickham was still accepted nearly everywhere, and he was a complete scoundrel. After talking to his cousin, he decided to speak to his aunt.

Lady Catherine was pleased to see him. "Darcy!" she said happily and set aside her deck of cards.

Darcy said, "I wish to speak to you about an important matter."

Lady Catherine said, "I knew it. When do you wish to set the date?"

He frowned. "I beg your pardon?"

"The wedding. When do you want to marry Anne?"

Darcy realized that he should have chosen his words better. "No, I am sorry, I do not want to speak of that. You already know my thoughts on that matter." He had told his aunt several times over the past few years that he did not wish to marry Anne, that he would not marry her, but she did not seem to listen to him.

She said, "I understand that you did not want to marry Anne when she was doing so poorly, but Dr. Moore says she is much healthier this Spring, and you must have noticed the bloom in her cheeks. She will make a lovely bride."

Anne looked more like a corpse with her thin arms and skeletal face. "No, ma'am. I am not going to marry your daughter."

"But it was the fervent wish of your mother. We planned the arrangement when you were both in your cradles."

She often said that, but since he was two years older than Anne, Darcy thought it unlikely that he had been in a cradle at the time. "I am sorry to disappoint you, but I do not wish to marry Anne and she does not wish to marry me."

"Have you asked her? Did she refuse you?"

"No, ma'am, but we discussed the matter years

ago. Neither one of us wish to marry. We are more like brother and sister."

"You are cousins," Lady Catherine argued. "And cousins marry all the time. Anne is perfect for you. She is your equal in birth, fortune and education. She will make an excellent mistress for Pemberley and later, when I am gone, she will inherit Rosings. What more could you want?"

I want Elizabeth Bennet, he thought, but had the sense not to say it. "Forgive me, ma'am. I don't wish to distress you."

Lady Catherine pouted. "I am most seriously displeased. Why must you be so disagreeable?"

Darcy said, "Let us speak of something else. I came to speak to you about Signor Bianchi."

"What of him?" Lady Catherine snapped.

"Perhaps it is merely his Italian nature, but he seems – shall I say – overly warm in his attentions to Anne."

"If you are jealous, that could mean that you are falling in love with her," Lady Catherine said triumphantly.

"Not at all," he said firmly. "And although I don't wish to condemn the man without evidence, I remember hearing something scandalous about his past."

"I have heard nothing," Lady Catherine said defensively. "And Lady Hodges gave me her recommendation."

"You must do as you see fit," Darcy said. "But I suggest that Mrs. Jenkinson keep a watchful eye."

"I will do better than that," Lady Catherine said. "I will dismiss him today."

"That seems drastic."

"Better to be safe than sorry," Lady Catherine said. "And it is not as if Anne was learning the pianoforte very quickly, anyway."

ANNE ACCOSTED Darcy in the stables when he returned from a ride. Darcy dismounted and handed the reins to a stable hand. "Anne," he said, alarmed by her pale face. "What is it? Is something wrong?"

"You!' she accused. "You had Signor Bianchi dismissed."

Darcy looked at the stable hands who gawked at them, interested in their conversation. "Let me walk you back to the house," he said and offered her his arm.

Anne's face was set in anger, but she took his

arm. Once they were away from the stables, Darcy said, "That was your mother's decision, not mine."

"But Mama would never have done it if you had not prompted her. How dare you?"

Darcy had never seen her so animated. Anger gave her face a surprisingly healthy glow. "I had heard something bad about him."

"Gossip. Nothing more," Anne said bitterly. "You should know better than to give it any heed. How dare you interfere? Those lessons were one of my few joys and now you have taken them away. I will never forgive you."

Suddenly she sounded more like his younger sister Georgiana than her usual quiet self. Darcy regretted the impulse that had made him speak to his aunt. "I am sorry, Anne. I would not wish to lessen any of your pleasures."

"If you were so concerned, why did you speak to my mother instead of me?"

Darcy felt foolish now. "I thought he was flirting with you.

"Would that be so terrible? I am twenty-seven years old. No one else has ever bothered to flirt with me before, but it is not a crime. I think you are like the dog in the manger. You don't want me, but you don't want anyone else to have me, either."

Darcy's conscience struck him. Perhaps she was right. "Are you in love with him?" he asked gently.

"No, of course not, but I enjoyed his attentions. They were completely innocent, Darcy, and you ruined it."

Darcy realized that after his sister's near elopement the summer before, he might be overly sensitive, seeing evil where none existed. "I don't know what more I can say."

"There is nothing to be said. He is gone and I will never see him again." Her voice broke.

Darcy felt like an ogre. Anne said she did not love Signor Bianchi, but obviously her heart had been touched.

Together they walked back to the house across a large lawn.

As they neared, Anne stopped for a moment to dry her eyes with a handkerchief. She said weakly, "I have nothing more to look forward to."

"The trip to Bath?" Darcy suggested.

"That is an ordeal, not a treat. I shall have to drink the dreadful water and sit around with my mother talking to ancient old goats."

The prospect sounded ghastly. "Perhaps you will find an interesting gentleman in Bath."

"A widower with six children?" Anne scoffed.

"Even if I did find someone who wanted me, Mama is determined for us to marry each other."

"I know. But perhaps if someone else appears to take your hand, she will abandon that idea."

"No, the only way she will let go of that dream is if you marry someone else. And even then, I wouldn't put it past her to poison your bride."

Darcy laughed, surprised by her dark humour. Anne had some hidden depths of feeling. He said, "I believe you are right."

Anne smiled at him grimly. "I am still mad at you, Darcy."

"I know. And I am sorry."

CHAPTER THREE

DURING THE WEEK after Mr. Darcy's morning visit, Mrs. Collins and Elizabeth saw little of either Lady Catherine or her daughter. No doubt they were engaged with their company. Colonel Fitzwilliam had called at the Parsonage more than once and Elizabeth had found him as agreeable as he had been at first. As for Mr. Darcy, she had only seen him at church at the services on Good Friday and he made no effort to speak with her. So much for Charlotte's theory that he was enamoured by her. But then on Easter-day, Lady Catherine spoke to Mr. and Mrs. Collins, inviting them and their guests to come to Rosings in the evening, so Elizabeth supposed she would see Mr. Darcy then.

"It will be for coffee only," Mr. Collins advised

Elizabeth as they walked back to the Parsonage. "Not for dinner, so we must eat before we go, Mrs. Collins."

"Yes, sir," Charlotte assured him. "I already have a meal planned."

"Excellent, Mrs. Collins. I should have known that you would have everything well prepared."

That evening, when they arrived in the drawing room, Lady Catherine did little more than acknowledge their presence. She was engrossed by her nephews, speaking primarily to them, especially to Darcy, much more than to any other person in the room.

In contrast, Colonel Fitzwilliam seemed really glad to see them. Elizabeth suspected that after nearly a week with Lady Catherine and Darcy, he must be starved for conversation. He seated himself beside Elizabeth and began to talk so agreeably of Kent and Hertfordshire, of travelling and staying at home, of new books and music, that Elizabeth had never been half so well entertained in that room before. Indeed, she began to think the evening might actually be enjoyable.

Elizabeth looked up to see Darcy watching them with a look of curiosity.

Lady Catherine must have felt the same, for she

called out, "What is that you are saying, Fitzwilliam? What are you telling Miss Bennet? Let me hear what it is."

"We are speaking of music, Madam," the Colonel said when he could no longer avoid a reply.

"Oh, of music!" Lady Catherine said. "Then pray, speak loud enough for all of us to hear you. Music is of all subjects my delight. I must have my share in the conversation, if you are speaking of music. There are few people in England, I suppose, who have more true enjoyment of music than myself, or a better natural taste."

At this, Miss de Bourgh suddenly stood up and swayed, looking as if she might faint. She started walking towards the door.

"Anne!" Lady Catherine demanded. "Where are you going?"

"Forgive me, Mama, I have a headache," Miss de Bourgh said quietly, but Elizabeth noticed that she had tears in her eyes.

Mrs. Jenkinson stood up to take her arm. "I will go with her."

"Yes, please do," Lady Catherine said, sounding annoyed.

Once Miss de Bourgh had left, Mr. Collins said, "Headaches are terrible, not only for their severity, but for their unpredictability, but your daughter has the patience of a saint. She bears her trials with such forti -"

"Yes, that is enough, Mr. Collins," Lady Catherine interrupted and Mr. Collins silenced.

Elizabeth looked between Lady Catherine, seeing her annoyance and Mr. Darcy, who looked concerned. Elizabeth guessed that there was more to the situation than either were saying.

Fortunately, coffee was then served, which provided some minimal conversation. Afterwards, Colonel Fitzwilliam reminded Elizabeth that she had promised to play for him. Elizabeth sat down at the instrument grateful for the respite. He drew a chair near her. Lady Catherine listened to half a song with her jaw held tight, and then she talked with Mr. Darcy until he walked away from her and drew near the pianoforte, stationing himself so he could see Elizabeth's face as she played.

"Do you mean to frighten me, Mr. Darcy," Elizabeth teased. "By coming in all this state to hear me?"

He smiled at her. "I doubt you are frightened. You have a natural courage that always rises to the occasion."

She was surprised by his compliment, not

certain how to take it. "We shall see how many mistakes I make, then."

The Colonel turned the pages for her and she played several songs. When she had finished, Mr. Darcy complimented her, saying that he had rarely enjoyed a performance more.

Lady Catherine said it was very pretty. She added coolly, "But you would play better, Miss Bennet, if you had the advantage of a London master."

"Ah yes," Mr. Collins agreed. "But not everyone has the advantages of your daughter, Miss de Bourgh. We cannot expect the same level of artistry from someone who does not have a tutor such as Signor Bianchi."

"I have dismissed Signor Bianchi," Lady Catherine said angrily. "And I shall replace him with someone better."

Mr. Collins swallowed nervously. "Considering your love of music, I expect no less and I am certain that Miss de Bourgh will flourish under her new tutelage."

Lady Catherine nodded, mollified by his flattery. A few moment later, she summoned her carriage to take the Collinses home.

THE NEXT DAY, Anne invited Darcy to join her for an al fresco luncheon. Al fresco was Italian for "in the cool air," and made Darcy think of Signor Bianchi. Normally Darcy was not fond of eating out of doors, but he felt guilty for depriving Anne of her music instructor, so he agreed. Anne drove them in her pony cart to the folly that Sir Lewis had built early days in his marriage to Lady Catherine. It was a large round pavilion with columns and a spherical roof. From the vantage point, they could look down on Rosings Park and much of the surrounding woods. "At least we will not get drenched if it rains," Darcy said.

He carried the basket that Cook had packed and Anne carried a blanket for them to sit on.

"Isn't this nice?" Anne asked, once the blanket was stretched out on the floor of the pavilion and the food unpacked. Anne had arranged for a selection of meat pies, cut fruit and salads.

Darcy much preferred eating in a dining room rather than half lying on the ground. He was not a Roman. "It is refreshing," he said and draped a large cloth napkin over his lap.

Anne sighed happily. "I think I would eat

outside every day, if I could." Although the day was warm, Anne was wearing both a pelisse and a shawl to avoid a chill.

Anne took a bite of a slice of apple. "I thought of inviting Miss Bennet today as well," she said casually.

Darcy startled. "Why?"

"She seems the type of girl who would enjoy eating al fresco."

She would, Darcy thought. She was a breath of fresh air compared to Miss Bingley.

"And I saw the way you watched her last night," Anne added with a smile. "Are you in love with her? Are you going to marry her?"

"Don't be ridiculous."

"Why is it ridiculous?"

"Because she is completely unsuitable."

"She seems very nice."

"She, herself, is absolutely wonderful, but her family and connections are not. And as much as the poets would have us think that love is most important, when you marry, you marry the person's family as well. There is no escaping that fact. And Elizabeth's family is impossible."

Anne was quiet for a moment. "I never realized how prejudiced you are, Darcy."

"I am a realist," he countered.

"You sound like my mother."

That set him back for a moment. He added, "To be honest, Elizabeth might not like our extended family, either. She has a delightful appreciation for the absurd and disregard for foolish traditions. She would hate the selfishness and artifice of London society."

"You hate London society, too."

"Yes, but I am willing to endure it when necessary."

Anne sighed. "I think it's a shame. I think everyone should marry for love, if they have the opportunity."

The topic of this conversation made Darcy uncomfortable, so he asked, "Is your headache better?"

She shook her head. "I almost always have a headache. It is a matter of degree only."

"I am sorry to hear it."

Anne shrugged. "I have spoken to specialists in London. They think I shall only live a few more years, possibly ten if I am very fortunate."

Darcy was shocked by her calm disclosure, but upon reflection, he realized that he had already suspected this. Anne had been so ill as a child, that once his own father said he was surprised that she lived to adulthood. "Does your mother know?"

"Mama knows, but she refuses to believe it. When she does not like what a physician says, she finds another physician."

That sounded like his aunt. "Perhaps that is her way of never giving up hope."

Anne smiled wryly. "Perhaps."

After a few moments, Darcy said, "Your mother is a difficult woman, but she loves you."

"No," Anne said. "I used to think that, but now I think that she only loves herself. I have been a great disappointment to her."

Darcy could not disagree. "So what are you going to do now? Is there anything you will do differently, knowing that your days are few?" He did not know what he would do if he thought death was around the corner, other than making certain Georgiana was taken care of and that Pemberley was in good hands.

Then the thought hit him – he would marry Elizabeth Bennet – regardless of the naysayers.

Why should he spend his life doing what everyone else thought was correct instead of doing what he knew in his heart was right?

For a moment, he was so full of hope and

happiness that he did not hear what Anne was saying. He did not know if she had answered his question.

He saw that she was filling a glass with punch. "This is for you," she said and handed it to him.

Darcy took a deep swallow and made a face at the excessive sweetness.

"Is something wrong?" Anne asked. "I made it for you myself, particularly for you."

He did not want to disappoint her. "It is fine," he said and forced himself to take another swallow.

The thick liquid seemed to catch in his throat and he coughed. Anne watched him with concern. He realized that she was not drinking any of the punch herself.

"Do you not want any?" he asked.

"No, not today," she said. "But please finish yours."

He took another swallow and thought his head felt strange. "I think I may have a headache, too," he said, then recognized the effects of laudanum. He gasped. "Anne, what have you done?"

"Tit for tat."

He frowned. Was this her revenge for getting her tutor dismissed? He felt as if he had never known her. "But why?"

"Carpe diem," Anne said.

Darcy tried to stand, but he staggered and slumped back to the ground. He groaned. As he drifted off into a deep slumber, he remembered the words of the Roman poet Horace.

Strain your wine and prove your wisdom. Life is short, should hope be more? In the moment of our talking, envious time has ebbed away. Seize the day, trust tomorrow even as little as you may.

Darcy hoped he would live to see tomorrow.

CHAPTER FOUR

ELIZABETH TOOK time nearly every day to walk the grounds of Rosings Park. She adored being outdoors where she could walk as fast as she wished, or sit on an old fallen branch and watch the leaves ripple in the wind without having to make polite conversation.

And today, the day after Easter, she had much to think upon.

The night before, Lady Catherine had been angry about something, and Miss de Bourgh had been visibly agitated.

Colonel Fitzwilliam had been his usual happy self, and Darcy had been more gracious than he had been in the past.

If it were not for Darcy's vicious behaviour with

Wickham, she might think him capable of becoming a civilized man.

She lifted her narrow muslin skirt and petticoat several inches so she could take longer strides. Her sturdy ankle boots became caked with mud, but she would brush them clean later.

As she turned back towards the Parsonage, she saw Miss de Bourgh approaching, driving a pony cart. "Miss Bennet," that young woman cried out. "Do you have time to play the pianoforte with me?"

Elizabeth was surprised by the invitation, for Miss de Bourgh had said very little to her in the past, but perhaps this was her attempt at friendship. Elizabeth said, "Yes, I would be happy to. Let me tell Mrs. Collins where I am going."

Miss de Bourgh hesitated. "To be honest, Miss Bennet, there is no time for that. For I have only an hour to myself before Mrs. Jenkinson returns for my German lessons."

Elizabeth smiled with sympathy. "Oh, dear."

Miss de Bourgh nodded. "My mother insists."

At that moment, Elizabeth was grateful that her mother had taken almost no concern for her education. "Very well," Elizabeth said and climbed into the cart with her hostess. "I suppose it won't matter.

Mrs. Collins knows I like long walks, so she will not expect me back for a while."

They drove up behind Rosings and past the stables. Miss de Bourgh stopped the cart by a back door. Elizabeth said, "Is this the servant's entrance?"

"It is a second entrance to the wine cellar," Miss de Bourgh explained. They both disembarked and Miss de Bourgh led the way to the door. Elizabeth adjusted her pace to match Miss de Bourgh's slower one. Miss de Bourgh said, "I discovered an old trunk down stairs, full of music sheets. The trunk is too heavy for me to lift, but I thought you might like to choose a piece from that."

"How intriguing," Elizabeth said. "It sounds like a hidden treasure."

"Yes, I thought you would enjoy seeing it."

Once inside the building, they both walked down a hallway and then down some stairs, their footsteps echoing. As the hall grew darker with shadows, Elizabeth asked. "Is there a light?"

"Forgive me, Miss Bennet," Miss de Bourgh said. "I am so accustomed to this part of the house, I forget how dark it is." Miss de Bourgh reached up to where there was a lantern and tinder on a hook on the wall. She lit the lantern. "Better now?"

Elizabeth nodded. "Yes." The stone stairway was narrow, so she stepped carefully so as not to slip. "I am surprised that someone would keep a chest of music in a cellar. Do you know who left it there?"

"Most likely my father," Miss de Bourgh said. "He was a very musical man. He played several instruments, including the violin."

They approached a heavy wooden door with a massive bolt and several locks.

Elizabeth shivered. "This looks a little like a dungeon."

Miss de Bourgh said, "My father was very particular about his wine collection. He had a friend whose home was robbed and he was determined that his precious collection would be safe."

Miss de Bourgh handed Elizabeth the lantern. "Please hold this, while I unlock the door."

Elizabeth held the lantern as Miss de Bourgh used three different keys from a large metal ring to open the door. Miss de Bourgh then held the door open for Elizabeth. "You first," she said. "The trunk is over to the left, behind the shelving."

Elizabeth stepped into the room, holding the lantern high. She saw that there was an open area with a large table that could easily seat a dozen.

This area was surrounded by rows of large barrels and beyond that, shelves that contained hundreds, possibly thousands of wine bottles. "Good heavens," she breathed out. "I have never seen so much wine in one place in my life." She looked back over her shoulder to ask Miss de Bourgh how long her father had taken to amass his collection, when she saw the door to the cellar closing.

"Miss de Bourgh?" she asked, thinking at first that her hostess was already within.

But then the door closed and she heard the locks being turned.

"Miss de Bourgh!" she shouted. "What is the meaning of this?"

"Forgive me," Miss de Bourgh said loudly.

Elizabeth heard the sound of the heavy wooden bolt sliding into place. She was trapped. "Please!" she shouted and banged against the door with her fists. "Let me out."

"I cannot," Miss de Bourgh said. "Not for a few days."

Days? Was Miss de Bourgh insane?

Elizabeth pulled at the door handle, but the door was secure and would not budge.

"You won't starve," Miss de Bourgh said, her

voice muffled through the keyhole. "There are meat pies."

Meat pies? The ridiculousness of her comment made Elizabeth want to laugh. Was this a dream? A nightmare? "Wait," she called out. "Don't leave me!"

"Good luck, Miss Bennet," Miss de Bourgh said.

CHAPTER FIVE

Elizabeth tried to open the door several more times, but then she stood for a few minutes, dumb-founded. How could this be happening to her? She felt as if she were suddenly living inside one of the gothic novels that Lydia liked to read with their dark castles, evil villains, and improbable plots. What was she to do? She then leaned, half-sat on the large table as she considered her options. Thank goodness Miss de Bourgh had given her a lantern, or her predicament would be much worse.

First, she decided she must survey her surround-ings. Miss de Bourgh had mentioned that this was a second door to the wine cellar, so that meant there was another door and perhaps it would be unlocked. And if not unlocked, perhaps someone would hear her if she beat upon it. Lady Catherine employed dozens of servants. Surely one of them would hear her and come to her aid.

Elizabeth walked throughout the cellar, amazed by the amount of wine and by the dust. She would have thought that Lady Catherine would have done a better job keeping the place tidy.

In addition to the central room there were several side rooms, all within a series of stone arches that held up the ceiling. There were a few windows at the very top of the ceiling, but they seemed too small to climb through and were covered by iron bars.

The floor was flat stone in some places, hard packed dirt in others. As Elizabeth searched for a door, she heard a scratching sound.

Rats, she thought and shuddered with distaste, but upon lifting her lantern higher, she saw a large yellow cat, licking itself clean. "Oh, you sweetheart," she said and set the lantern down carefully. She reached out to pet the animal, not wanting to frighten it. But the creature seemed tame and after a few minutes, allowed her to pick him up. Elizabeth buried her nose in the animal's warm fur, grateful that she would not have to spend her time in the cellar alone.

The cat purred as Elizabeth stroked him.

"I wish you could tell me the way out of here," Elizabeth said. Eventually she set the cat back down, picked up the lantern and resumed her tour. She saw a door at the end of a hallway, but there was a rolled carpet or bag in the way. As she neared, she saw that it was not a carpet, but a body.

Elizabeth cried out and shrank back. The sound of her cry echoed throughout the cellar, but there was no response. Elizabeth gathered her courage and stepped closer. But as she came to see the man more clearly, she recognized him. It was Mr. Darcy.

"Good Heavens," she gasped and leaned down to see him more closely. Was he dead?

She touched his face and blessedly his skin was still warm. She listened and heard his steady breathing. He was alive.

She shook his shoulder. "Mr. Darcy," she said firmly. "Please, Mr. Darcy, awake. There has been an accident."

He opened his eyes and stared at her with dazed eyes. "Darling girl," he murmured in slurred tones, then closed his eyes again.

Darling girl? Either Mr. Darcy was inebriated, or he had been drugged. She shook his shoulder again. "Mr. Darcy. I need your help."

She managed to rouse him a second time, but he muttered what sounded like "go away" and pushed at her with one of his hands, so she decided to let that sleeping dog lie.

She stepped past him to the door at the end of the hallway, but as she had suspected, it was locked, and no one came when she called and beat upon the door.

So she sat down on the dusty floor, several feet away from Mr. Darcy, out of arm's reach, and waited.

Darcy appeared to have been drugged, but otherwise he appeared unharmed.

But the entire situation made no sense. Why would Miss de Bourgh trap them both within the wine cellar?

Now if it had been Miss Bingley, Elizabeth might have understood, for that young woman had always seemed devious and unkind. If she thought Elizabeth was gaining Mr. Darcy's attention, she would gladly lock Elizabeth in a dungeon and throw away the key.

But for Miss de Bourgh to wish her ill? And to punish Darcy as well?

That did not make sense.

Elizabeth wondered how soon she would be

missed. What would Charlotte think when she did not return from her walk?

Elizabeth sighed. Her mother had often complained about her solitary walks, always wanting her to take one of her sisters. "One of these days, you will have a mishap!" she had warned.

Her father had dismissed her fears. "Lizzy can take care of herself," he had said.

Elizabeth hoped that would be the case now, but she did not know what to do.

If she was discovered having spent hours in a locked room with Mr. Darcy, her reputation would be ruined. Unless, perhaps she could find a way to escape before he woke.

She looked at him, lying in an ungraceful slump. Despite his awkward posture, he was a handsome man with his thick dark hair, noble nose and square jaw. And he did not look as imposing when asleep. He looked younger, more approachable.

After half an hour, it occurred to her that she might be able to pick a lock with one of her hairpins, but another hour proved that was impossible.

The lantern light flickered and Elizabeth feared that she would eventually be in the dark. She looked through the cellar and found a supply of candles and flint. She lit several candles and set them on candle holders on the large table. At least she would be able to see.

She also found a basket filled with fruit and meat pies. She had to laugh. Her jailor had been generous, but that also meant that the decision to imprison her had been carefully planned.

She ate one of the pies and waited for Darcy to wake.

Mrs. Collins began to worry when Elizabeth did not return to the Parsonage in time for tea. She sent one of her servants, James, to walk along the paths to look for her. He returned an hour later and said he had not seen her.

Mrs. Collins spoke to Mr. Collins. "I believe something has happened to Elizabeth. Perhaps she has fallen and injured herself."

Mr. Collins said, "What do you want me to do — organize a party to search for her?"

"Yes, that would be most kind."

"I think you are overly concerned," Mr. Collins said. "Cousin Elizabeth is fond of walking and I believe she will return before dinner."

But she did not and Mr. Collins became irritated by his wife's looks of concern. "She should have taken a maid with her - or Mariah," he said sharply. "It is not safe for young women to traipse about by themselves. When she does return, I will give her a stern talking to."

"Yes, Mr. Collins," Mrs. Collins agreed. "But first, let us find her. She is a guest in our house, and we should care for her safety."

After dinner, Mr. Collins announced that he would go to Rosings Park. "Lady Catherine will know what to do," he said.

"What are you saying?" Lady Catherine demanded of Mrs. Jenkinson before dinner. "Anne is gone?"

"Yes, ma'am. I thought she was resting instead of taking tea, but when I went to her room to check on her, her bed was made and there was a letter addressed to you."

Lady Catherine hastily opened the sealed letter.

Dearest Mama,

Do not be concerned for me, for I am well. Darcy and I have decided to elope to Gretna Green. We cannot wait to become man and wife.

You have wanted this union for so long, we knew you would not mind terribly if we took matters into our own hands.

And when we return, you can host a celebration.

Please be happy for me.

Anne

LADY CATHERINE HELD the letter against her breast. Anne marrying Darcy? It was the most fervent wish of her heart. But why an elopement? She remembered Darcy saying that he would not marry Anne. Perhaps he had been too proud to share his real feelings with her.

But if word got out, there would be a scandal.

Lady Catherine considered sending Colonel Fitzwilliam after them, to insist that they return and marry at Rosings, but then she thought better of it. No, it would be wiser to let those two impetuous romantic fools run their course. She would hush up as much gossip as she could.

She turned to Mrs. Jenkinson.

"Anne is fine," she said. "But I will need you to create the fiction that she has remained at Rosings. You are to stay in her bedroom and pretend that you are caring for her."

Mrs. Jenkinson said, "Yes, ma'am."

After Mrs. Jenkinson left, Lady Catherine sent for Darcy's valet, Mr. Bowles. "I understand that Mr. Darcy was called away on business," she said.

Mr. Bowles was surprised. "Not that I know of, ma'am."

"He informed me of the matter," Lady Catherine said stiffly. "I assume he will return within a week or so. Naturally, you may stay until he returns."

"Yes, ma'am."

Mr. Bowles sought out Colonel Fitzwilliam who was reading in the library before dinner. "Sir," he said. "May I speak with you a moment?"

"Yes, what is it Bowles?" the Colonel replied.

"Lady Catherine has informed me that Darcy has been called away on business."

The Colonel frowned. "I know nothing of that."

"Nor do I," Bowles said. "And Mr. Darcy did not take so much as a portmanteau."

"Did he take any change of clothes?"

"No, sir."

The Colonel said, "That is not like him. Darcy is a methodical man, certainly not one to act hastily."

"No, sir."

The Colonel said. "Thank you for telling me. I will investigate the matter further."

Later at dinner, when the Colonel asked Lady Catherine about Darcy's plans, she said sharply, "I am sure he does not tell you everything, Fitzwilliam. Every man has secrets – even my late husband Sir Lewis had a few. I believe we should let Darcy do what he wishes and wait for his return."

"Yes, ma'am," the Colonel said.

Lady Catherine took a bite of her ragout and smiled. Anne would be Mistress of Pemberley. All of her dreams for her daughter were coming true.

But she was quite annoyed later that evening, during coffee, when Mr. Collins appeared to speak with her. He apologized for bothering her for several minutes, then he told her of Elizabeth Bennet's disappearance.

Lady Catherine's first thought was that Anne might have brought Miss Bennet along to Gretna Green to act as a chaperone, but since she did not know that for a certainty, she gave Mr. Collins permission to use some of her servants to search for his guest.

"Thank you, ma'am. Your generosity is unparalleled." He bowed and scraped.

Colonel Fitzwilliam rose to his feet. "Let me assist you," he offered.

Lady Catherine said, "But you have not finished your coffee, Fitzwilliam."

The Colonel drained his cup and set it down sharply. "Now, if you will excuse me, ma'am." He bowed.

Lady Catherine waved her hand at him. "Do what you wish, but I believe it will all come right in the end."

The Colonel walked out of the room with Mr. Collins. "When was the last time anyone saw Miss Bennet?"

CHAPTER SIX

DARCY FELT as if he were walking through fog and his head ached. He opened his eyes and saw that he was in a dark room, lit only by candlelight. And for some reason he was lying on the floor.

A feminine voice asked, "Are you awake now?"

He blinked. That sounded like Elizabeth Bennet, but what was she doing in his bedroom?

He peered at her closely. It was Elizabeth.

Shocked, he tried to sit up, but his head swam. "Forgive me," he said after a moment. "I don't understand. Where am I?"

"In the wine cellar."

This did not make sense. He must still be dreaming. But he yawned and stretched and sat upright and she was still there, observing him with her fine eyes.

She wore a rumpled day dress and her hair was untidy. "Miss Bennet?" he asked.

She nodded. "As you see."

"I don't understand," he repeated.

"Neither do I," she said calmly. "But apparently, you were drugged and placed here. And Miss de Bourgh locked me in here as well."

Memories of their outdoor luncheon came back to him. "She laced some punch with laudanum," Darcy said. "But why?"

"I have no idea," Elizabeth said. "You as her cousin might know better. Is she mad?"

"Not as far as I know, but her actions today certainly raise the possibility." Darcy rose to his feet. "Are we locked in?" he asked.

"Yes. I tried for several hours to escape with no success."

"Let me see what I can do." He took one of the candles and walked over to the locked door. He pulled and pushed but the door remained locked. He banged on the door and shouted, "Help! Please help us!"

There was no response.

Elizabeth said, "Surely someone will hear you."

He shook his head. "Perhaps not. The cellar is hidden away. In the normal course of a day, no one would pass by."

"Not even to fetch wine for dinner?" Elizabeth asked.

Darcy looked at his watch fob. "It is past dinner time now. From what I understand, there is another room nearer the kitchen for daily wines. This cellar is more for Sir Lewis' collection."

She nodded. "And he has made it very secure."

Too secure, Darcy thought. He removed a small knife from his coat pocket and attempted to pick one of the locks.

Elizabeth stood by his side, waiting. "I tried that as well, but I did not have a knife."

After half an hour's effort, he abandoned the attempt. "Is there another door?"

"Yes," she said and walked with him to show it. "This is where I came in. Miss de Bourgh and I came from the back gardens."

Darcy tried to force this door as well with no luck. He struck the strong wooden panels and shouted. This time, Elizabeth joined in as well. "Help!"

But after a few minutes, it seemed futile to continue to shout.

He dropped his hands to his sides and sighed. "It seems we are trapped here, Miss Bennet."

She said, "Miss de Bourgh mentioned that it would only be for a few days."

"Days?" he repeated.

"Yes, sir."

"Then at least she has some plan of releasing us, but that does not lessen our predicament."

Her dark eyes acknowledged the truth of his words. "I know."

She knew as well as he what the ramifications would be.

He straightened his shoulders. He knew his duty and he would not shirk from it. He said, "I had hoped to have this conversation at a later date, but I suppose I should speak now and lessen your concerns. Miss Bennet," he said formally, "Would you do me the great honour of accepting my hand in marriage?"

She blanched. "I beg your pardon?"

"I am asking you to marry me."

"But why?"

"Why now? Because your reputation will be ruined."

"Not if we can find a way to escape."

"I think you know better than that. Once it is

learned that we have spent the night together, people will talk."

"I hate gossip," Elizabeth said, her voice tight.

He reached out to take her hand. "So do I, but rest assured, that is not the only reason I am asking you to marry me. Today's events merely sped up the timing of my proposal." He ran his thumb over the knuckles of her hand in a gentle caress. "You must allow me to tell you how ardently I admire and love you."

She looked stunned. "You love me?"

"Yes. I have loved you for months, but I fought against it." It seemed so ridiculous now, but he needed to explain his motives. "I worried about your family and your low connections. I thought that my friends and family would not accept you. But now, considering our situation, there is no other choice. Fate, aided by my Cousin Anne, has forced my hand, and I have never been happier." He smiled down at her. "I will do my best to be an excellent husband."

She pulled her hand away from his and stepped back. "Please sir," she said, when he would have followed her. "Do not press me."

He stood back. "No, of course not. I will not

take advantage of our confinement." As much as he greatly wished to kiss her, he would refrain.

She nodded. "Thank you."

He watched with growing concern as she remained silent. She stood apart from him, her hands folded in front of herself, her face solemn. "Elizabeth?" he prompted after a minute.

She said, "Forgive me, sir, but your proposal has shocked me and I do not know how to reply."

"Say yes, of course."

She smiled grimly. "That is easy for you to say because apparently, it will give you what you want – my hand in marriage. But although you profess to love me, I do not believe you. I overheard you tell Mr. Bingley that I was not handsome enough to tempt you."

Darcy felt a rush of embarrassment. "I am sorry you heard that. At the Assembly, I was in a foul mood. I did not want to dance and I did not want Bingley's teasings. I am sorry I insulted you. But I have repented of my hasty words and I now consider you one of the handsomest women of my acquaintance."

She held up her hand as if to stop him. "Since the Assembly, you have only spoken to me a handful of times and most of the time you have glared at me. You don't know me at all."

"I do not have the talent of conversing easily. Especially in crowds," he admitted. "But my heart is true. I love you, Elizabeth."

"But I do not love you, sir."

He was momentarily taken aback by the vehemence of her words. But he respected her honesty. "I am sorry to hear that, but I believe that in time, love can grow between us." He knew of countless couples who had begun their marriage with only affection.

"I doubt it."

He frowned. "Have I done something to offend you?"

At this she laughed out loud. "When have you *not* done something to offend me?"

None of this made sense. He struggled for composure. "Please tell me what I have done. I thought from our conversations that you were anticipating my address."

She turned on him. "I should not be surprised by your misreading my feelings. I assume that as a man of wealth and consequence, you are accustomed to having women fawn over you. But I am not one of those women."

"No, and that is why I value your good opinion."

"If you wanted my good opinion, you should have behaved better."

"In what way?"

"In countess ways. Your manners are stiff and proud and you act as if you do not care for the feelings of others. But if you wish for particulars, I can begin with Mr. Wickham. He told me of your dealings with him. How can you defend yourself on that matter?"

Now Darcy was offended that she had believed the tales of that blackguard. "You take an eager interest in that gentleman's concerns."

"Yes," Elizabeth said hotly. "I do. Who that knows of his misfortunes could help but feel an interest in him?"

Darcy felt a surge of jealousy. Did Elizabeth care for that villain? He remembered that she had championed him at the ball. "His misfortunes have been of his own making!"

"And how is that? You are the one who denied him a living. You have reduced him to his present state of poverty, comparative poverty."

Darcy clenched his hands into fists as he struggled for composure. "And this is what you think of me!"

"Yes, I do."

He said finally, "I don't know what lies Wickham has told you, but I will tell you the truth."

She looked at him defiantly as if to say, 'go ahead.'

"No, not here," he said. "Let us find a place to sit down. It is a long story." Together they walked back to the large open area where there was a table. Darcy searched several rooms until he found two chairs and set them at the table.

Elizabeth sat across from him and waited.

"What do you know of George Wickham's past?" Darcy asked.

"He said that he was the son of your father's steward and that you grew up together at Pemberley."

"That is true. His father was a very respectable man who had for many years the management of all the Pemberley estates. I don't think he knew, just as my father never knew, George Wickham's true nature."

"And what nature is that?"

Darcy looked at her, wondering how much detail

he should give her, and then decided to give it all. There was no question that they had the time to discuss it fully, and he hoped that if he were completely honest that she would believe him. And, if Elizabeth were to become his wife, he would want no secrets from her. He said, "Wickham has intelligence and a quick wit. He is personable and most people like him at first, until his lies become known. He is careful to hide his selfish and immoral tendencies. He drinks to excess, gambles beyond his means, I suspect often cheating, and runs up bills he has no intention of paying. And worst of all, he takes advantage of women – frequenting brothels or flattering young women into thinking he cares for them."

Elizabeth gasped. "Why is this not known?"

"Who is going to accuse him?" Darcy countered. "Many men admire a Don Juan, and servant girls don't want to lose their positions."

Darcy continued. "When my father died five years ago, he left Wickham a legacy of one thousand pounds and desired that a valuable family living become his when it became vacant. But Wickham told me he had resolved against taking orders, and I knew he ought not to be clergyman, so we settled the matter. He resigned all claim to that living and accepted in return three thousand pounds."

Elizabeth said, "So much?"

"Yes, and one day, you can see the papers if you wish."

"No, I believe you," she said quietly.

"Wickham expressed an interest in studying the law, but nothing came of that, and later, when the living became available, he requested it, reminding me that it had been my father's wish." Darcy frowned, remembering Wickham's conceit. "I refused, which infuriated him, and I can imagine he told many people of my unfair treatment. After this, I did not see or hear from him for months, until last summer when he most painfully reappeared in my life."

"What happened?"

"This is part of my tale that I would rather not share, for it involves my younger sister Georgiana. She is more than ten years my junior, and I am her guardian, along with Colonel Fitzwilliam."

Elizabeth looked concerned. "Did Wickham harm her?"

He nodded. "But fortunately, it was not as bad as it could have been. My sister attended school in London and last summer she went with the lady who presided over it, a Mrs. Younge, to Ramsgate. Wickham visited her, undoubtedly by design, for we later learned that he had a prior acquaintance with Mrs. Younge. Together he and Mrs. Younge schemed, and he convinced Georgiana to fall in love with him and to agree to an elopement."

"Oh no," Elizabeth breathed out.

"She was only fifteen, which must be her excuse," Darcy said flatly, remembering those dark days. "But I joined them unexpectedly a day or two before the intended elopement, and Georgiana, not wanting to upset me, told me all. You may imagine what I felt and how I acted."

"Your poor sister."

"Yes. Wickham fled the county and I dismissed Mrs. Younge."

"Do you think he cared for your sister at all?"

"No. He cared for her dowry, which is thirty thousand pounds. And I believe he also acted to revenge himself upon me. If he had taken Georgiana to Scotland, his revenge would have been complete."

Elizabeth said, "I am glad you stopped him."

"So am I."

"Was your sister very unhappy?"

"She cried for weeks, but she appears better

now. We spent Christmas together and she went back to school. A different school, obviously, and she writes me daily."

Elizabeth nodded, as if deep in thought.

Darcy asked, "Do you believe me now?"

CHAPTER SEVEN

Eᴌɪᴢᴀʙᴇᴛʜ ᴅɪᴅ ɴᴏᴛ ᴋɴᴏᴡ how she felt – her mind was in a tumult as she listened to Darcy. Who was the villain - Wickham or Darcy? Elizabeth wanted to dismiss Darcy's charges of Wickham's extravagance and general profligacy, but there was an air of truth about him, particularly in regards to his sister Georgiana. Surely Darcy would not lie about her.

And she could muster no proof to support Wickham's innocence. She had never heard of him before his joining the militia at Meryton. Of his former way of life, nothing had been known, but what he told himself. As to his real character, she had no real knowledge. His countenance, voice, and manner had given the impression of goodness and she had believed that without question.

She tried to recollect some instance of goodness, some distinguished trait of integrity or benevolence that might counterbalance Darcy's claims, but there was nothing.

And in looking back, she could now see the indelicacy of his Wickham's prior behaviour – how he had aired his woes to her whereas Mr. Darcy had been more circumspect. And Wickham had boasted of having no fear of Darcy, but then he had chosen to avoid the Netherfield Ball. And most damning - he had waited until Darcy had left Hertfordshire before telling everyone else how he had been mistreated. He had no scruples in sinking Mr. Darcy's character, when Darcy was not present to refute his claims.

In contrast, Darcy's reputation was more well-known. He had an excellent friend in Mr. Bingley and Elizabeth knew from his comments that he cared for his sister.

"I do believe you," she told Darcy finally.

"Thank you."

For a few minutes, Elizabeth sat silently, absolutely ashamed of herself. She realized that she had been blind, partial, prejudiced and absurd. She had misjudged Darcy because he had insulted her, and she had believed Wickham because he flattered her. It was embarrassing to realize how foolish she had been.

She who had always prided herself on her discernment.

It was all vanity now.

She looked at Darcy who seemed lost in his own thoughts as well. She said, "Wickham recently became engaged to Miss King. At the time, I was surprised because he had not shown any interest in her. But now I know he wants her because she inherited ten thousand pounds."

Darcy smiled dryly. "Only ten? He must be feeling desperate."

Elizabeth felt sorry for Miss King, but she did not want to talk about Wickham any longer. She said, "Do you think anyone will miss us and begin to search for us?"

"Perhaps Colonel Fitzwilliam will wonder where I am. And what about you?"

"Mrs. Collins will worry when I don't return. All she knows is that I went for a walk."

Darcy smiled. "You always were an excellent walker. I remember when you arrived at Netherfield to see your sister Jane."

Elizabeth said, "I know I looked very untidy that morning. It was rather muddy after the rain."

"You were so lovely, you took my breath away," Darcy said.

Elizabeth looked down.

"Do I embarrass you?"

"A little," she admitted. "I would rather you did not flatter me."

"It is not flattery if I tell the truth."

Elizabeth felt herself blush. She did not know how to react to Darcy's obvious approval. She still could not believe that Darcy had proposed to her and that she had misunderstood his attentions. Charlotte had been correct after all.

And although she still did not want Darcy as a husband, she was flattered that she was his choice. She was pleased that a learned, wealthy man who could choose almost any woman in the country wanted her.

Poor Miss Bingley, she thought, and smiled wryly.

"What is it?" he asked. "What amuses you?"

"I am thinking of Miss Bingley."

Darcy nodded. "She can be amusing, but only in hindsight. It is incomprehensible how an intelligent, amiable man like Mr. Bingley can have two such unpleasant sisters."

Elizabeth was surprised to learn that she and Mr. Darcy did have something in common. She said, "I agree. I think it may be due to their education."

"Or lack of it," Darcy commented. "I believe that if you take one capable young woman, and subject her to several years of Mrs. Whitmore's School for Young Ladies, and she will be become silly and pretentious. A dangerous combination."

Elizabeth thought of her younger sisters Kitty and Lydia who were silly and ignorant. She did not know which combination was worse.

She stood suddenly, tired of sitting. She began pacing about the main open area and swung her arms for the exercise. She said, "I hate sitting here, just waiting. What will happen if we are not discovered?"

"Well, with all the wine, we won't starve, although we may become foxed."

Elizabeth smiled at his attempt at humour. "Oh, I forgot to tell you. Miss de Bourgh left us some meat pies in a basket." She pointed to a basket resting by the base of one of the columns.

"No, thank you," he said politely. "I had one at luncheon and have no need for another."

Elizabeth who had already eaten one of the pies herself, agreed. She said, "They are not tasty, but they are filling." She continued to walk back and forth.

Darcy watched her idly and occasionally smiled at her when their gaze met.

After a few minutes, he said, "If you could choose any meal, what would it be?"

She looked at him quizzically. "I beg your pardon? Are we speaking hypothetically?"

"Come now, Miss Bennet," he said. "We are going to be in each other's company for hours, possibly days. We might as well talk."

"About anything?"

"Anything and everything, as you wish. I am at your command."

"You astonish me."

"Why?"

"I have always found you to be taciturn." Indeed, it had been a point of quiet humour to her, to mock his awkward silences.

"I am often reserved in public. It is difficult to converse with those I have never seen before. I cannot catch their tone of conversation or appear interested in their concerns as I often see done. I am much more comfortable in conversations that are one-to-one. And over time, as I get to know some-one, and to trust them, I can speak more freely."

His admission of a personal weakness surprised her and made her rethink some of her prior opin-ions. Instead of being arrogant, was Mr. Darcy shy? "Do you trust me, Mr. Darcy?" she asked archly.

He said seriously, "I love you. And by offering marriage, I have offered you all of myself – heart, mind, body and soul, so I should hope that I trust you."

Elizabeth, suddenly uncomfortable with the depth of his sincerity, held up her hand. "Please, sir. I would rather speak of food than love."

He nodded. "As you wish."

His eyes looked at her so warmly that for a moment, Elizabeth was too flustered to speak, but then she gathered her wits and said, "My favourite meal would include soused lamb, sole, a salad and a very large pudding."

"Do you have a sweet tooth?"

"Yes, but I try to limit myself. When I was younger, my mother would discourage us if we took more than one serving. She would say 'Careful, girls. You don't want to become as large as Sir William."

"Sir William Lucas," Darcy said, remembering. "That is Mrs. Collins' father."

"Yes."

"He is a massive man, but not quite as large as Prinny."

Elizabeth was surprised. "Have you met the Prince?"

Darcy said, "Yes, on several occasions, but I do not run in his circles."

"Thank goodness for that," Elizabeth said.

"You do not approve of the Prince Regent?"

Elizabeth said, "It is not my place to approve or disapprove, although I think his behaviour to Mrs. Fitzherbert is shocking and I pity Princess Caroline."

He nodded. "Arranged marriages are rarely happy ones. But as much as I disapprove of the man's morals, I am more concerned about his extravagant expenses."

Elizabeth found it interesting as Darcy discussed the politics of their day. In her home, her father subscribed to several newspapers, but he rarely discussed their content with her, and her mother was more interested in fashion and local gossip.

It occurred to Elizabeth that one advantage of marrying Darcy would be to learn more about the world.

But she did not want to think of that. She changed the subject. "Tell me about Pemberley."

"What would you like to know?"

She thought of Mr. Collins telling her Aunt Phillips the cost of one of Lady Catherine's chimney pieces. "When was it built?"

"Seventeen twenty-two."

"Brick?"

"No, stone mostly, silver white. It is very pretty in the morning sun."

"Tell me more," she prompted and he described it to her, using his large graceful hands to illustrate his words.

"It has a large rectangular basement on the ground floor, and then the piano nobile contains the principal rooms. Above that are bedroom attics. Each of the four corners has a small tower. Original plans were for domes like those of Houghton Hall, but fortunately my ancestor had better taste."

Elizabeth smiled as he expected her to.

He continued, "Then there are two lower flanking wings connected by colonnades. And to the south of the house there is a stable block."

"It sounds lovely," she said. As he spoke, she realized the difference in their station. Longbourn was a comfortable country home, but Pemberley sounded more like a palace.

"It is, but I think you will particularly enjoy the grounds. The estate has three thousand acres, and one thousand of those are in a parkland arranged by Bridgeman. There is a stream that has been enlarged into a little lake. There are two paths around the parkland – the longer being ten miles around."

"How often do you walk the larger path?" Elizabeth asked.

"Not as often as I should," he admitted. "When I was younger, I ran it."

"Ten miles?" she repeated, impressed by his athleticism. "I should like to see that." In the summer, there were often footraces in Meryton, but she did not know of anyone who could run ten miles.

He looked at her, his eyes gleaming in the candlelight. "Agreed. But if I succeed, I'll want a prize."

She realized he was flirting with her, looking at her lips as he spoke.

She shivered. Who was this Mr. Darcy and what

had happened to the odious man she had known before?

Somehow the hours of their confinement and the long conversation in the candlelight had softened him.

Elizabeth had noticed before the effects of late hours and candlelight. She and Jane spoke often in the evenings, and it seemed easier to converse openly late at night, in a quiet house when everyone else was asleep. Elizabeth yawned behind her hand and asked, "What time is it?"

Darcy opened his watch that hung from a fob on his waist. "It is almost midnight."

CHAPTER EIGHT

Mrs. Collins spoke to Colonel Fitzwilliam on the doorstep of the Parsonage. "You did not find Miss Bennet?"

"No, ma'am," the Colonel said. He wore a long frock coat and he looked weary. His chin, usually clean shaven was now dark with stubble. "And it is too late now to continue. But in the morning, we shall resume our search and speak to all of Lady Catherine's neighbours."

"Do you think she was abducted?" Mrs. Collins asked.

The Colonel shook his head. "I think it more likely that she was injured somehow and that she wandered off. I have seen it on the battlefield."

Mrs. Collins thanked him for his efforts.

He said, "Do not give up hope. We shall find your friend."

Mrs. Collins said, "Mr. Collins told me that Mr. Darcy also left unexpectedly today."

"Yes, that is what Lady Catherine says."

"Do you think –" Charlotte said, then caught herself, not wanting to give word to her scandalous thought.

"That they might be together?" the Colonel finished quietly. "Perhaps. It is certainly a mystery, and hopefully one that will be solved soon."

Mr. Collins approached the two of them. "Good night, Colonel," he said briskly. Once the front door was closed, he turned to Mrs. Collins. "You should go to bed immediately Mrs. Collins or you will be unable to manage my breakfast."

DARCY WATCHED ELIZABETH INTENTLY. There was so much he wanted to say to her, feelings he wanted to share, but she was skittish. She did not want him to talk of love, so he would be patient and talk of other things. He said, "Tell me about your family. In truth, I cannot keep the names of your younger sisters straight."

She looked at him with amusement. "Why does that not surprise me?"

He smiled.

"Jane is the eldest and then I follow her. Mary is next. She is the one who also plays the pianoforte and sings."

Darcy frowned. "I remember."

"She often chooses songs that are beyond the capacity of her voice, which makes me wonder if she is slightly deaf. Surely if she understood how she sounded, she would not be so eager to perform. She also likes to read serious, philosophical books and quote passages."

She sounded like one of Darcy's cousins. He asked, "Does anyone listen to her?"

Elizabeth seemed surprised by the question. "Not really," she said, and then her face brightened. "I think that is the problem. For years my mother has dismissed Mary as the plainest of her daughters and generally has little use for her. I think you are right that poor Mary has done what she could to be noticed. I am ashamed that I never noticed before. Once we are free and I return home, I will spend more time with her."

Elizabeth had a kind heart. "What about your other two sisters?"

"Catherine, or Kitty as we call her, follows Lydia's lead. She does not read much or think much, actually, except about dancing and officers but she likes animals, particularly horses."

"And Lydia?"

"She is the loudest of my siblings and the most active. She cares little for society's rules, finding them stupid. You have seen her. She is impulsive and often selfish. I used to worry that she would do something to ruin us all, but it seems I am the one who will ruin us all – and through no fault of my own."

Darcy's heart was touched. "Do not worry about that. I will take care that your reputation is not harmed."

"Thank you, I know you mean to be kind, but I still wish our situation was different." Elizabeth returned to the original topic of their conversation. "Lydia is my mother's favourite, just as I am my father's favourite." Elizabeth made a face. "I don't think it is wise for parents to have favourites. Even if one has a preference, I believe parents should keep that knowledge to themselves and strive to love each of their children."

"I agree," Darcy said. "My parents did not have favourites, at least as far as I could tell. My sister and I were both spoiled, though. Our parents thought we could do no wrong."

She looked at him closely. "So that is why."

"Why what?"

She shook her head. "Do not worry, I am just trying to understand you better."

"You will have a lifetime for that," he said. "Just as I will have a lifetime to learn all about you."

He could see that his words made her uncomfortable. She smiled slightly and said only, "We shall see."

ELIZABETH RUBBED her eyes and hid a yawn behind her hand. It was getting late and she was tired. She and Darcy had talked about their childhoods and their favourite books, anything and everything except the topic on both of their minds – what would happen when they were discovered. Or worse, if they were discovered. If they were not discovered, would they starve to death?

For her peace of mind, Elizabeth had to believe what Anne had said – that they would only have to be in the cellar for a few days, but what did that mean?

As for their reputations, Darcy thought they would marry, that they must marry.

And as the hours passed, she began to fear that he was correct. She knew the way of the world. Everyone would talk. Once she was free, if she returned to Longbourn, everyone would stare at her belly, wondering if she was already with child.

Even if she did marry, all the gossips would count months on their fingers between the wedding date and any birth.

She watched as Darcy walked around the cellar, looking at various bottles, occasionally wiping off a handwritten label to read the contents. He chose two, brought them back to the table and uncorked one with opened with a pop sound. "Would you care for a drink, Miss Bennet?" he asked.

She looked about. "Are there no glasses?"

"None that I can see. And there is nothing else to drink."

He handed her the bottle and she brought it up to her lips. Tiny bubbles of air teased her nose as she sipped. "Ah, sparkling wine," she said.

He nodded. "Champagne. Sir Lewis has an excellent collection."

"I never understood how champagne gets its bubbles."

"It is from a second fermentation where sugar is added."

Mr. Darcy had a wealth of information. She smiled at him and took another sip. "Whatever the scientific reason, it is delicious."

He motioned to the room. "And we have no fear of running short."

She laughed at that. "Are you trying to get me foxed, Mr. Darcy?"

"That depends upon your reaction."

She thought for a moment. "On the few occasions when I have consumed too much wine, I get a headache and am sleepy."

He nodded. "When I drink too much, I become morose, or so Bingley tells me. He, on the other hand, becomes giddy."

Elizabeth said, "Truly?"

"After the Netherfield ball, we stayed awake later, drinking and talking and he ended up with a fit of giggles."

That was an amusing mental picture, but Elizabeth did not comment. She was not sympathetic towards Mr. Bingley at the moment. The autumn before, Mr. Bingley had moved into Netherfield Park, an estate only three miles from her home. Mr. Bingley was a single young man with a fortune of four thousand pounds a year, an eligible catch. For several weeks, it had seemed as if Bingley preferred her oldest sister Jane, the sweetest, most beautiful girl in England. He often singled her out for conversation and had danced with her as often as propriety would allow. And most telling, he had postponed scheduling his ball until Jane was well enough to attend.

Her mother had thought he would propose at any moment.

And Jane, dear Jane who never thought ill of any one and who would never offend anyone, had fallen in love with him.

But then, after the ball, Bingley left for London with plans of returning within a week. But he did not return and as the weeks passed, Jane, although she would never admit it, began to lose hope that he would ever return. Mrs. Bennet had sent Jane to London to visit their Aunt and Uncle Gardiner with the hope that Jane would somehow meet up with him.

But that had not happened. Miss Bingley had come to call at the Gardiners once, but Mr. Bingley had never called.

Elizabeth thought now that Bingley was like most young men – foolish and fickle.

She took another sip of the champagne.

She decided that she liked champagne very much. She was beginning to feel more relaxed and hopeful. Surely they would be discovered in the morning.

After a few minutes, Darcy excused himself and took a candle with him.

Elizabeth wondered if he had gone in search of something that could be used as a chamber pot. She was beginning to think that she would need something as well. She frowned at the inconvenience and potential embarrassment. Miss de Bourgh had thought of food, but had not prepared for all eventualities.

Darcy returned, saying, "Elizabeth, come see what I have discovered."

She noticed that he had used her first name, but perhaps after all they had shared it was ridiculous for him to continue to call her Miss Bennet. She took her own candle and followed after him. "What is it? Have you found a way to escape?"

"No, but I have found something very interesting.

He led her to a tiny room behind a panelled wood wall. "Look at this. It is a secret room."

It was a small room with a desk, chair, bookshelves and a small rope bed. Everything was tidy, but the air inside was dusty as if it had not been inhabited for years.

"It was hidden?"

"Yes. I pushed against one of the panels by accident and the door opened slightly.

Elizabeth took about the room. "What could be its purpose?"

"I think this was where Sir Lewis de Bourgh came to escape from Lady Catherine."

Elizabeth smiled. Gothic novels often had secret rooms, and she was relieved that this one was harmless with no chains on the walls. She said, "How clever, but it is very sad, too."

He nodded. "I know. I remember when I was a child that Lady Catherine often complained that Sir Lewis would disappear for hours at a time. He would politely apologize, but never explain where he had been, saying only that he was busy about estate business. I suppose he was in this little room, hiding."

Elizabeth bent down to read the selection of books on the bookcase and saw that most of the books were poetry. "Was Sir Lewis a romantic?"

"I don't know," Darcy said. He ran his hand over the spines of a set of leather-bound volumes.

He chose an early one and glanced through it. "These are his diaries," he said. "Listen to this," he said after a minute of perusing its pages. He quoted, "*The Darcys are visiting. Scamp Fitzwilliam dislocated his shoulder. He is lucky he did not break his head.*"

"Scamp?" Elizabeth teased. "Were you a scamp?'

"Hardly," Darcy said. "I was a very well-behaved boy, but I was fond of climbing trees. And I think that in comparison to Anne, I would seem mischievous."

"Did your shoulder heal?"

Darcy nodded and motioned with his arm. "Good as new. I have never had trouble with it."

Darcy looked through the diary for other interesting passages and after reading one page, his face paled. He sat down on the chair beside the desk as if his legs were weak.

"What is it?" Elizabeth said.

Darcy read aloud, "*I sat with Lady Anne in the rose gardens today for half an hour. I could not help but think of prior days and curse the ill-luck of a locked library door. Does she ever miss me, I wonder?*"

Elizabeth said, "What does that mean?"

"I think it means that Sir Lewis was once in love with my mother, Lady Anne."

"You think so?"

Darcy set the diary aside. He rested his chin on one hand. "It makes sense now. As a child, I occasionally overheard things that I did not understand. Lady Catherine often boasted about the gifts Sir Lewis bought her as if that proved his love for her. Sir Lewis always looked embarrassed and would either change the subject or leave the room. And once, when I was a young man, my mother warned me about making certain I was never alone with an unmarried young woman. She told me that one of her suitors found himself locked in room with someone else and was forced to marry her."

"Good heavens," Elizabeth breathed out. "The poor man. Do you think your mother loved Sir Lewis?"

Darcy shook his head. "I don't know. I don't think so. My parents seemed to love each other, but they married three years after Lady Catherine married Sir Lewis. But what does one ever know about another's private life?"

Elizabeth nodded. "I believe my parents cared for each other in the beginning. My mother was pretty and vivacious. But over the years, they have grown apart. My father has a more serious, studious nature and my mother can be silly and nervous. But

I think if he had taken more of an effort to educate her or if he were more patient, they could be happier now."

Darcy said, "There are so few happy marriages. I think I have seen less than half a dozen in London."

"I don't have your breadth of experience, but I agree," Elizabeth said soberly.

For a moment they looked at each other, neither of them speaking. If she married Mr. Darcy, could she be happy? Elizabeth wondered.

She was not in love with anyone else and he professed to love her.

It was all so vexing. She was furious with Anne de Bourgh for trapping them, and she could not help but wonder if Anne knew her parents' history. Had she locked them in together as her mother had once been locked in with her father?

Had she done this to force Darcy's hand?

If so, he did not seem to be very upset by it. Did he truly love her?

She tried to imagine being married to him, letting him kiss her and perform those mysterious marital acts that resulted in babies. She and Charlotte had discussed hypothetical possibilities when they were younger, but once Charlotte married Mr.

Collins, Elizabeth had not felt comfortable asking her friend for intimate details. After seeing some of the farm animals and some classical paintings, Elizabeth thought she had a fairly accurate idea of what was involved, but she knew that a theoretical idea would always be different from reality.

She looked at Darcy, noticing how large he was, broad through the shoulders with a strong chest that narrowed down to slim hips. As he sat, she could see the muscles of his thighs outlined by his smooth fitting pantaloons. She looked back at his face, which was shadowed by his beard now. She admired his straight nose and square jaw. She glanced briefly at his lips and wondered how it would feel to kiss him. She thought that she might feel better about marrying him if he would kiss her once. But then she blushed when he returned her steady gaze. She looked down, grateful that he could not know what she was thinking.

After a moment, Darcy cleared his throat. "At least, there is a bed now."

Her eyes flew open in shock.

"So you can rest, Miss Bennet," he continued and she took a deep breath to relax. He patted the rope bed and a cloud of dust arose from the blanket. "It may be dusty, but I believe it will better than the floor."

Elizabeth looked around. "And where will you sleep, sir?"

"I don't know if I will sleep," he said. "I will try the doors a few more times."

Elizabeth looked at the rope bed. She was very sleepy. "Very well," she said finally. "Thank you."

CHAPTER NINE

ELIZABETH WOKE IN THE DARK. Her first thought was confusion, wondering where she was and why her body ached. But then she remembered. She had spent the night in the wine cellar at Rosings Park. She felt around her bed, searching for a candle. The candle beside her had gutted out and the rope bed had been very uncomfortable. She sat up and saw at some time during the night that Darcy had covered her with his coat jacket. "Mr. Darcy?" she called out.

He appeared in the doorway of the little room, carrying a lit candle. "Good morning, Miss Bennet," he said politely. It was strange to see him in shirt sleeves and waistcoat and he had removed his cravat. His jaw was covered with dark stubble now and she could see some of the curling dark hairs on his chest in the small open v at his neck.

Good heavens, she thought. She had always seen him neatly shaven and did not realize how hairy he could be.

He asked, "Did you sleep well?"

"I did," she said, although it was an exaggeration. "And you?"

"I dozed a bit at the table."

She nodded and wondered how terrible she looked. She reached up to touch her curly hair, which had mostly fallen down now. "I don't suppose you have a comb on your person?"

"Unfortunately not," he said. "But rest assured, you look charming."

Elizabeth laughed. "Liar."

He sat beside her on the chair while she removed the remainder of her hair pins and combed through her tangled hair with her fingers. There was no hope for her long hair but to braid it, then twist it into a bun at the base of her neck and try to secure it again with the pins.

"I wish I had a mirror," she said. She was surprised by how comfortable she was with him. Spending so much time together had made their conversation easier.

"Would you like breakfast?" he asked, when she had finished with her hair.

"What is available?"

"Meat pies, if you are brave."

"I am certain that if we are here several days, I will eat another."

"And under the pies I found a few apples." He produced one dark red apple with a flourish.

She was pleased. "Much better."

She thought he would hand her the apple and let her eat it, biting it off the core like one of the stable hands, but instead, Darcy brought out his small knife and proceeded to peel the apple and then cut it into slices for her. "Thank you," she said.

As he handed her a slice, he would then wait while she ate it, then cut her another. Elizabeth thought she had never tasted anything sweeter. With the fruit, they drank a light wine, again directly from the bottles. "No champagne?" she teased.

"No, I thought it best if we save that for a celebration."

"And what will we be celebrating?"

"Our liberation."

Of course, he was as anxious as she to be released from their prison. She sighed. "I wonder what everyone is thinking."

"They might think we have eloped," he said. "And in truth, once we are released, that might be easiest. To just travel up to Scotland and take care of it without the bother and delay of getting a license. A *fait accompli*."

Elizabeth was surprised by how calm she felt. She was beginning to accept her inevitable fate — that of marrying Mr. Darcy. She did not love him, but the past day made her think that they might be able to work together amicably. She said, "If we must marry, I want my family to be there."

"Very well," Darcy agreed and smiled at her. "We can get married at Meryton, if you wish. I don't know if my uncle, the Earl of Matlock, will attend, but you will get to meet my sister Georgiana."

For a moment, she feared what his family would think of her. "Is the Earl of Matlock very grand?"

He smiled. "Imperious at times, but not half as grand as Lady Cathcrine."

Elizabeth smiled as well. She continued, "And I assume Bingley will come back to Netherfield, although I don't think Miss Bingley will be pleased to hear of our marriage."

"No," he agreed. "Perhaps it would be best if we marry at Pemberley and I don't invite Bingley."

"Why not?" Surely Miss Bingley's thoughts were irrelevant at a time like this.

"I don't think it wise for him to spend more time with your sister."

"What are you saying?"

Darcy shrugged. "Bingley likes your sister too much."

"I don't understand. Why should he not like her?"

"Well, apart from the disadvantages of your family and connections, and the impropriety of their behaviour, which you yourself acknowledge, Jane doesn't seem to care for him."

"Not care? She is in love with him."

Darcy looked astonished. "She does? Then if that is true, I am sorry that I contrived to keep them apart."

Elizabeth suddenly felt her heart grow cold. "Contrived? How? What did you do?"

"Let me explain. At the ball, I overheard Sir William Lucas mention the possibility of Bingley's marrying Jane as a certain event, with only the timing to be decided. I was surprised and decided to observe Bingley more closely. I saw that his partiality for your sister was great, but that hers was not equal to his. Your sister's manners were open, cheerful and engaging, but she had no special regard for him. And throughout the evening, I saw that although she received his attentions with pleasure, she did not invite them. She appeared indifferent."

"Indifferent?" Elizabeth demanded. "My sister is reserved. She does not show her feelings to the world, but she feels them deeply, and she loves your friend."

"Then I was mistaken. I misjudged her serene countenance."

"And what did you do?"

"I travelled with Bingley to London after the Ball and gave him my opinion."

Elizabeth snapped, "That my family was atrocious and that Jane did not like him."

Darcy did look a little embarrassed. "That was the gist of it, yes."

Elizabeth could not bear what she was hearing and for a moment she was too angry to respond. "And Bingley was so weak-willed that he let you persuade him to stay away?"

"Bingley has a natural modesty and a stronger dependence on my judgement than on his own."

"Then he is a fool."

"Perhaps I overstepped the bounds of our friendship, but I meant well."

"Overstepped?" Elizabeth repeated angrily. "You did more than that. You have ruined the happiness of my dearest sister and your friend. By separating them, you have exposed Bingley to the censure of the world for caprice and instability and exposed Jane to its derision for disappointed hopes."

"I admit that I may have been mistaken, but what I believed was based on calm impartial observation. I did not intend to harm either of them. I meant to help."

Elizabeth threw up her hands. "Spare me your excuses. Who were you to be the judge in this matter? Why did you think you should decide how Bingley was to be made happy? You are, without the doubt, the most arrogant man of my acquaintance."

"I can speak to Bingley again," he offered.

"What and tell him now that Jane loves him? Do not bother. Why would she want such a puppet?" Elizabeth turned away from him. "No, it is impossible. I should not be surprised by your actions. From our first meeting, I knew that you were insufferably proud. Your manners, your speech, everything about you shows your arrogance and conceit, and your wilful ignorance for the feelings of others. I was a fool to think you had changed or that you could be better."

"What are you saying?"

She turned to face Darcy. "I am saying that I don't like you, Mr. Darcy. And I won't marry you, no matter what anyone says." She refused to be like Sir Lewis, miserable in his marriage, hiding away in his basement.

"You don't have a choice." His words were harsh, his voice tight.

"That is where you are wrong. I do have a choice, and I would rather have my reputation ruined than accept your hand in marriage."

CHAPTER TEN

Colonel Fitzwilliam and a number of Lady Catherine's servants approached each of her neighbours, searching for Elizabeth Bennet with no success. By that evening, he said to Lady Catherine, "I think it is time for someone to write to Miss Bennet's parents."

"I think this is too much fuss," Lady Catherine said. "I am certain she will turn up eventually."

"I will speak to Mr. Collins," the Colonel said briskly. On his way to leave, he met with Mrs. Jenkinson in the hallway.

"Excuse me, sir. May I speak to you for a moment?"

Mrs. Jenkinson was an older woman, tall and thin, dressed in a dreary brown dress with white lace at the neck. The Colonel said, "Yes, certainly. Is it about Anne? I understand she has been ill, but with the confusion of both Darcy and Miss Bennet's disappearances, I have not visited her."

"Oh no," Mrs. Jenkinson said. "Miss de Bourgh is fine, or I should say, I assume that she is fine. But I am worried about Mr. Darcy and Miss Bennet."

"Everyone is worried," he said kindly.

"No," Mrs. Jenkinson explained in a quiet voice. "You see, I know where they are." She held up a ring of keys to the wine cellar. "Miss de Bourgh wanted me to wait at least two full days, but I dread thinking of them alone in the dark."

The Colonel gaped, astonished by her words. "But why would she do this?"

"She wanted time to elope with Signor Bianchi. She knew that if Lady Catherine thought she was with Mr. Darcy, she would not pursue them."

That made some kind of sick sense. "So Anne is gone?"

"Yes, she left yesterday afternoon."

"I never realized that Anne could be so devious," the Colonel said. "But first, let us free them."

"Not I," Mrs. Jenkinson said, shrinking back. "I don't want to anger Lady Catherine."

The Colonel took the keys from her hand.

"Very well, but if they have been harmed, I will hold you partially responsible."

"Miss de Bourgh gave Mr. Darcy some of her laudanum that she uses for her headaches, but she promised she would not give him too much."

The Colonel swore and hurried down to the ground floor. He asked directions to the wine cellar and walked down another set of stairs to a massive wooden door. He lifted the bolt and began to use the keys to open the door.

Within minutes the door was open and he carried a lantern into the darkness. "Darcy?" he called out. "Miss Bennet?"

DARCY HEARD HIS COUSIN CALLING. "Miss Bennet!" he said happily. "We are saved."

Elizabeth stood with her arms folded across her chest, refusing to speak to him. She had not spoken to him for the last few hours, once she had learned that he had separated Bingley from her sister Jane.

At first, Darcy had thought that her anger was unreasonable, particularly after his apology, but as the silence between then lengthened, he considered her words.

She did not like him. She thought he was so arrogant that she would prefer social ruin to becoming his wife.

That was a bitter lesson.

He did think highly of himself. It was second nature to himself. He had been spoiled by his parents, who thought he could do no wrong. He had been taught correct principles, but was left to follow them in pride and conceit. Until Elizabeth's rejection he had no reason to think that he was not the superior person he assumed he was.

It had never occurred to him that she could reject him. In his vanity, Darcy had thought that she was expecting his proposal. Then when she first denied him, it was because she had believed Wickham's lies. That was offensive but understandable. But once he told her the truth about Wickham, he assumed that she would see him as he was and gladly accept him.

But she did not want him.

He was unable of pleasing the only woman he wanted to please.

"Darcy!" Colonel Fitzwilliam cried heartily. "Good to see you. And Miss Bennet, are you well?"

Elizabeth said, "Well enough, but I will be glad to leave this place."

"Certainly, ma'am," the Colonel said and offered his hand to escort her up the stairs. "How did you get here?" he asked.

"Miss de Bourgh tricked me and then locked me inside."

"And she drugged me with laudanum," Darcy said as he slid his arms back into his coat. He did not bother with his cravat. "But I don't know why."

The Colonel said, "My understanding is that she has eloped with Bianchi, but she told Lady Catherine that she had eloped with you."

"Good heavens," Elizabeth said.

Darcy said, "Machiavelli de Bourgh?"

The Colonel smiled. "Precisely."

"How did she get me down stairs?" Darcy asked. "There is no way she could have carried or dragged me."

The Colonel said, "Bianchi was waiting outside in the woods beyond the Folly. Mrs. Jenkinson told me their plan."

Darcy's jaw tightened. "I like him even less than I did before."

Elizabeth asked carefully, "I understand Miss de Bourgh's desire to deceive her mother, but why did she lock me up as well?"

"Perhaps to strengthen her position," Darcy

answered. "By putting you in the cellar with me, she made certain that we would marry, making it impossible for me to marry her."

"But I am not going to marry you," Elizabeth said flatly.

The Colonel looked at Darcy with inquiring eyebrows but kept his silence.

Darcy merely shook his head. It did not matter what Elizabeth said. Ultimately her family would make her see reason. Together the three of them walked up the stairs to the main floor of the house.

Lady Catherine's cook looked as if she might faint. "Mr. Darcy!" she exclaimed. "And Miss Bennet!"

It was obvious that they had both been in the cellar a long time with his beard and their rumpled clothing. Within hours, gossip would spread through Rosings and into Hunsford. Darcy straightened his shoulders and said to a footman. "Please inform Lady Catherine that I wish to see her in the east drawing room."

"Yes, sir," that young man said sharply.

Darcy turned to Elizabeth. "I suggest you stay here with my cousin until after I speak with Lady Catherine."

"I want to go back to the Parsonage," Elizabeth said.

"I will take you later," Darcy promised. As he left the room, he heard the Colonel say, "Get ready for the fireworks!"

Lady Catherine, when she saw him, closed the door behind her with a slam and demanded, "Where is Anne?"

"I presume she is somewhere on the road to Scotland."

"But you are supposed to be with her."

Darcy stood his ground. "I don't know what she told you, ma'am, but I did not elope with her. I have spent most of the past two days locked in your wine cellar."

Lady Catherine paled and for a moment, Darcy felt some sympathy for her. "But why? If she did not go with you – with whom did she go?"

"Possibly with Signor Bianchi."

Lady Catherine closed her eyes and swayed for a moment as if she might swoon. But then she gathered her courage and said briskly, "This is unacceptable. I insist that you track her down this instant, Darcy, and bring her home."

Darcy said, "I cannot, for I have other obligations to Miss Bennet."

"Miss Bennet?" she cried. "What has she to do with anything?"

"Your daughter locked her in the wine cellar with me."

At this, Lady Catherine sat down on a settee. She was silent for a moment, then said, "No one need know about that. I can keep my servants quiet."

"No, ma'am," Darcy said. "I will do my duty to Miss Bennet. We spent the night together and I will marry her."

"Do not let your chivalry overcome your common sense, Darcy. No one will accept her as your wife. If you marry her, she will be censured, slighted and despised by all your friends."

"Then they are not my friends."

"Your alliance would be a disgrace. No one in the family will accept her."

Darcy looked at closely. "They accepted Sir Lewis."

Lady Catherine drew her breath in sharply. "What are you suggesting?"

"I am suggesting that my current situation is not unlike yours."

"Who told you?"

Darcy remained silent and she added angrily,

"Our situations are nothing alike. Sir Lewis was a knight and a man with property."

"And Miss Elizabeth Bennet is the daughter of a gentleman."

"But consider her relations. She has uncles in Trade."

Darcy realized how petty her arguments sounded and was embarrassed that he had ever thought the same. "She will be my wife, ma'am. Whether or not you acknowledge her is your decision, but it will not affect my ultimate happiness."

"Then you are determined to have her."

He looked at her directly. "Yes, I am."

"And what about Anne? Will you do nothing to save her?"

"Colonel Fitzwilliam can go after her, if you wish. But personally, I think it would be better to let her have some happiness. Anne won't live long, but if you are fortunate, perhaps she will have a baby."

"A baby at Rosings," Lady Catherine said, her face brightening. "I never thought of that. Do you think it is possible?"

"I don't know. Perhaps you should speak to her doctor."

"I know," Lady Catherine said. "Perhaps we can

imply that Signor Bianchi is a nobleman who left Italy under an assumed name."

Darcy shook his head at this new nonsense. "Good day, ma'am."

IF ELIZABETH HAD NOT BEEN SO TIRED after her adventure, she would have found her conversation with Mr. Collins that evening amusing. As it was, she was eager to get to her own bed and try to forget all the excitement. Mr. Darcy had walked with her to the Parsonage. Charlotte greeted her with a hug and worries about her health. When Mr. Collins heard that Elizabeth and Darcy had spent the night in the wine cellar, he was horrified. "What does Lady Catherine say?"

"She has other concerns," Elizabeth assured him.

Mr. Collins did not know what to think. He turned to his wife for guidance. "Do you think it proper, Mrs. Collins, to let Cousin Elizabeth stay in our house after she has spent the night with Mr. Darcy?" Do you think she would be a bad influence upon your sister Maria?"

At this, Darcy said stepped forward to face him.

"If you are implying that anything untoward occurred, you may say it directly to me and face the consequences."

"Mr. Darcy, please don't challenge him to a duel," Elizabeth said dryly and Mr. Collins blanched.

"I do not believe in violence, sir." Mr. Collins stammered.

"No, but I do," Darcy said darkly. "And I trust you will not mention or refer to our time in the wine cellar again."

"Oh no, sir," Mr. Collins said. "My lips are sealed. I would not in any way want to besmirch the reputation of my dear cousin or the nephew of my patroness."

"Thank you," Darcy said. He turned to Elizabeth. "We shall travel to London in the morning. I don't know yet if the Colonel will accompany us."

"You will need a chaperone or at least a maid to travel with you, Cousin Elizabeth," Mr. Collins reminded, but as Darcy's eyes narrowed with a dangerous glint, he added, "But perhaps it does not matter now, given your particular circumstances. She shall be packed and ready to leave in the morning, sir. My wife shall make certain of it."

Later, once Mr. Darcy had said good night and

Mr. Collins had retreated to his study, Charlotte hugged Elizabeth again and said, "I was so worried."

"So was I," Elizabeth confessed. "I was afraid that no one would find us, but Colonel Fitzwilliam came to our rescue and all is well now."

Charlotte looked at her closely. "You know you'll have to marry Mr. Darcy."

Elizabeth refused to acknowledge that. She hoped against hope that somehow her father or Uncle Gardiner would be able to save her. She could think of nothing worse than to answer to Mr. Darcy for the rest of her life

"Are you hungry?" Charlotte asked. "I have some meat pies in the pantry."

Elizabeth laughed. Meat pies again? "No, thank you. I will eat breakfast tomorrow."

CHAPTER ELEVEN

THE NEXT MORNING, Elizabeth sat in Darcy's carriage, facing him and Colonel Fitzwilliam as they travelled from Kent to London. Mr. Bowles sat outside with the driver. Colonel Fitzwilliam tried to keep up a steady stream of pleasant conversation, but Elizabeth was in no mood to talk and spent most of the time staring out the window.

Every rotation of the carriage wheels brought her closer to London and closer to her home. Her father had supported her in her refusal of Mr. Collins, but would he support her refusing Mr. Darcy?

Her father would not care for Mr. Darcy's fortune, but she feared he would care about her reputation and the gossip that would surround her.

She was afraid of the gossip as well, but she was more afraid of being married to a man that she could not love or respect. At heart, Mr. Darcy was a conceited, arrogant man accustomed to getting his own way. For a few hours in the cellar, when they were both trying to escape, she had softened towards him, seeing him in a better light. But then when she learned of his actions separating Bingley from Jane, she was reminded of his true nature.

She remembered the way he had treated nearly everyone in Meryton when he first came to Hertfordshire. Her parents, her friends, and even Sir William Lucas had been beneath his notice. It would break her heart to be on the receiving side of his disdain as well.

This week he might think that he loved her, but how long would that last? Her parents' love had not lasted. Also, he might defer to her now, as a tactic to win her approval, but down the road, she feared that he would slip back into old patterns of tyrannical behaviour.

After four hours, they arrived at the Gardiners' house in Cheapside.

Mrs. Gardiner was surprised to see her. "Lizzy!" she exclaimed. "I thought you would stay with your friends another week at least. Is everything all right?"

Elizabeth said, "Not exactly, but first let me introduce you to Mr. Darcy, who brought me here."

Introductions were made and to her surprise, Mr. Darcy was very polite to her aunt. Mrs. Gardiner apologized for her husband's absence for he was currently at his warehouse. She said that he would be sorry he had missed them, but that she could send a servant to fetch him if necessary

"No, there is no need. I will call again tomorrow morning," Darcy said formally. "And at that time, I hope to be able to speak to Mr. Gardiner privately."

Mrs. Gardiner's eyes widened, but she said merely that it would be a pleasure.

After that, Darcy said his farewells and took his leave.

"Well," Mrs. Gardiner said, once he was gone. "I never thought I would speak to Mr. Darcy face-to-face. I knew his father by reputation, years ago, when I lived in Lambton, but we were never acquainted. I was surprised by his civility today, after you had said he was so disagreeable, Lizzy. I recognize that there is something stately in his manner, but I would not call it pride precisely. More a matter of confidence."

Elizabeth admitted, "He is not always disagreeable."

"I am glad to hear it. But I will still be on my guard with him, because I remember how he treated poor Wickham."

Elizabeth was embarrassed by all the things she had said last December. She said, "I have learned more about those matters, and I believe we should not trust everything Wickham told us."

Jane said, "I knew there must be some explanation. Mr. Bingley would not have Mr. Darcy as his closest friend if Mr. Darcy was unprincipled."

Mrs. Gardiner said, "I suppose Mr. Darcy was travelling in this direction and offered you a ride?"

"No, there is more than that," Elizabeth confessed. She quickly explained the entire situation to Mrs. Gardiner and Jane of how they had been locked in the wine cellar and then their rescue more than a day later. "Oh, Lizzy," Jane said. "That must have been terrifying."

"Actually, it was not as bad as it sounds," Elizabeth said. "But it was awkward."

Mrs. Gardiner shook her head. "It is a bad business, Lizzy."

Elizabeth nodded. "I know, but what am I to do about it?"

"Marry him," Mrs. Gardiner said bluntly. "If he will take you."

Elizabeth shook her head. "It is so unfair. Nothing improper happened. All we did was talk and drink some champagne. He didn't even kiss me."

"I am glad to hear it," Mrs. Gardiner said. "It shows he is principled and self-disciplined."

Or that he did not find her attractive. Elizabeth was not certain she believed Darcy's protestations of love. They seemed conveniently timed, possibly a ruse to save himself the humiliation of being forced to marry her. "He has proposed," she said finally.

"Excellent," Mrs. Gardiner said just as Jane said, "How can you marry him when you dislike him?"

Elizabeth said, "I have refused him."

At this, Mrs. Gardiner tsked her tongue. "You are too sensible for that, Lizzy."

Elizabeth did not feel sensible. She was unhappy and felt ill-used. If she were Lydia she would throw a tantrum and stomp upstairs to a bedroom, slamming doors, but there was no point in that, so she merely said, "I will try to be wise."

Mr. Gardiner when he returned from his work, also spoke to her. "I will speak with Mr. Darcy in the morning and I hope he will have reasonable plans. After I speak to him, I will write to your father and together, we shall determine the best course. We will take care of you, Lizzy."

Elizabeth did not want to be taken care of. "Do I have no say in the matter?" she asked.

Her uncle smiled at her and patted her arm. "Of course you do," he said kindly. "But you are young and not fully aware of the risks and conse-quences involved. It is our responsibility to guide you."

That was what worried her.

In the morning, Mr. Darcy appeared on the Gardiner's doorstep at ten o-clock, with Mr. Bingley at his side. Both were dressed in their best day attire, from their brilliant white cravats down to their polished boots. Elizabeth had heard once that some gentlemen put champagne in their boot polish, but she doubted that Darcy would be so ridiculous.

Mrs. Gardiner was gracious as she welcomed both gentlemen into her home and the introduc-tions were made. Elizabeth glanced at Jane to see her reaction. Jane blushed and smiled and looked down at her hands in her lap as if she could not bear to look at Mr. Bingley directly.

But then Mr. Bingley spoke to her, explaining that he had only recently learned that she was in Town.

Elizabeth glanced at Mr. Darcy, who was more quiet than his friend. He nodded as if to say, "Yes, I told him."

After a few minutes of small talk about weather and the health of their respective families, Mr. Gardiner joined them. After several pleasantries, Mr. Gardiner said, "Mr. Darcy, would you care to join me in my office?"

Darcy looked briefly at Elizabeth and it was her turn to blush and look down. She felt as if everyone was staring at her, for everyone knew why Darcy was going to speak to her uncle.

He was there for half an hour. When he returned, he asked Elizabeth if she would go riding with him in his curricle that afternoon.

Elizabeth nodded. "Yes, sir."

Encouraged by Darcy's success, Bingley asked Jane if he could take her for a ride as well.

After both gentlemen left, Mr. Gardiner said,

"Mr. Darcy is a sensible man. He is perfectly well behaved, polite and forthright."

"I agree," Mrs. Gardiner said. "The more I see of him, the more I like him."

Elizabeth thought it a pity that she did not feel the same.

Mr. Gardiner added, "Mr. Darcy thinks it best if he takes you and Jane down to Longbourn as soon as possible, leaving tomorrow morning, and I agree."

"Very well. I will make certain my trunk is packed," she said calmly, but inwardly she was seething. This was yet another example of Darcy making all the decisions without consulting her. It did not auger well for their future together.

During their ride that afternoon, they stopped at Darcy House in Cavendish Square. Darcy wished her to come inside briefly to meet his sister Georgiana – a sweet, shy girl, but Elizabeth also wondered if he was showing her one of his properties to persuade her to accept his proposal. When pressed for her opinion on Darcy House, Elizabeth agreed that it was lovely. When he said, "I hope you will enjoy living here when we are in Town," she reminded him that she had not yet accepted his proposal.

"I can wait," he said cheerfully.

Odious man.

Elizabeth had a headache by the time the drive ended and when she returned, she went up to the bedroom where she was sleeping to avoid Mrs. Gardiner's questions.

Jane joined her half an hour later with good news. "Oh, Lizzy," she exclaimed after hugging her. "I am the happiest woman in the world. Mr. Bingley loves me. He says he has always loved me, but when he left Netherfield last November, he thought I did not care for him and that is why he did not come back. But now that he has seen me again, he wants to marry me. He is travelling back tomorrow and will speak to our father."

"I am happy for you," Elizabeth said honestly, although she thought Jane was too nice to forgive Bingley so quickly. How would the man truly appreciate her if she did not stand up for herself?

Jane took her hands. "And I want you to be happy as well. Do you think you can come to love Mr. Darcy? I believe he means well, and it would be so wonderful for your husband and mine to be friends."

Elizabeth changed the subject by asking Jane to

tell her everything Bingley had said when he proposed.

That evening, Mrs. Gardiner spoke to Elizabeth privately. "I am sorry to see you and Jane go so soon, but I suppose we will all meet again for the weddings. Perhaps you can have a double wedding."

"I have not yet decided whether I will marry Mr. Darcy," Elizabeth said.

Mrs. Gardiner said, "What other choice do you have?"

"Could I live with you?" Elizabeth asked.

Mrs. Gardiner said, "As much as I love your company, I cannot approve of that plan. Your reputation will be ruined and it might even affect Mr. Gardiner's business."

Elizabeth nodded. She hadn't thought of that. She supposed that her vague plans of becoming a governess or working in a shop selling bonnets were equally impossible. "I just don't want to marry Mr. Darcy. I am afraid that as a husband he will be a despot." From her observation, most men were petty tyrants.

"A wise woman learns to work with her husband."

"Does Mr. Gardiner tell you what to do?"

"Sometimes," Mrs. Gardiner admitted and then she smiled, "And sometimes I tell him. But truly, Lizzy, if he loves you, he will want you to be happy."

Elizabeth said, "You don't know the worst of it. He was the one who kept Bingley from Jane. Back in December, he convinced Bingley to stay in London rather than return to Netherfield. He did it to keep Bingley from proposing to Jane."

Mrs. Gardiner frowned. "I don't understand. If that were the case, why did he bring Mr. Bingley to our house to see her?"

"He only did it because I told him that Jane cared for Mr. Bingley."

Mrs. Gardiner said, "Then it looks as if you are already learning how to influence him for the better."

Elizabeth said, "That is not the point. What infuriates me is that he interfered, thinking he knew best."

"Most men think they do know best," Mrs. Gardiner reminded. "Yes, even your uncle. And dare I say it – you often think it yourself."

Elizabeth smiled wryly. "You are right. I am not conciliatory. It is not in my nature. I am afraid that if we married, Mr. Darcy and I would be at loggerheads, always arguing. I don't want a man who orders me about or worse, who does whatever he wants without consulting me." She feared that if she married Mr. Darcy, he would ignore her and she might lose herself, like Charlotte.

"None of us can foresee the future," Mrs. Gardiner said. "And you know how to express yourself without giving offense."

Elizabeth sighed. "I just want to be happy, as you and Mr. Gardiner are."

Mrs. Gardiner laughed, "Oh dear. Do you think we were as well-matched when we first wed? Absolutely not. I cried too much over small mishaps and he spent too much time at his business, never talking to me about his concerns. But over the years, as we talked and shared our lives, we grew closer until now I believe we could finish each other's sentences."

Elizabeth said, "What is the secret to a happy marriage?"

Mrs. Gardiner said, "I think the Bible says it best: Charity suffereth long and is kind. Charity envieth not. Charity vaunteth not itself, is not puffed up. Doth not behave itself unseemly, seeketh not her own, is not easily provoked, thinketh no evil. Rejoiceth not in iniquity, but rejoiceth in the truth.

Beareth all things, believeth all things, hopeth all things, endureth all things. Charity never faileth."

"That sounds as if the wife must do all the giving."

"Oh no, the husband must have charity, too."

They spoke for a few more minutes and Elizabeth expressed her unhappiness with Mr. Bingley for being so easily persuaded to give up Jane. "I don't know if I will ever forgive him for being so malleable."

Mrs. Gardiner said, "If Jane can forgive him, why can't you?"

That evening, as Elizabeth lay in a bed she shared with Jane, unable to sleep, she thought over the past few days – days that had forever changed her life.

Normally she was not formed for ill-humour. She rarely dwelt long on her sorrows and she could find humour in almost any situation.

Indeed, even now, she knew her mother would be shocked and consider her a candidate for Bedlam for even considering to refuse a man worth ten thousand pounds a year.

Elizabeth sighed and adjusted a feather pillow, trying to be comfortable. Her aunt was correct. Her objections to Mr. Darcy were not merely that he separated Jane from Bingley. Her fear was that he might not truly love her. That he might be selfish and unkind, as so many men were.

Marriage was a risk that terrified her, especially a marriage formed only to avoid scandal.

Darcy had said once that he had a resentful temper. That his good opinion once lost was lost forever. What would happen if she ever displeased him? Would he forgive her?"

Could she learn to love him or like the Bible verse must she merely learn to endure him?

CHAPTER TWELVE

THE BENNET FAMILY were as disagreeable as Darcy remembered – particularly loud and disorganized – but since he now planned to marry Elizabeth, Darcy was determined to be civil, to show Elizabeth that her reproofs had been attended to. He wanted to lessen her ill opinion, so he sat silently in the Longbourn sitting room as her mother and sisters exclaimed over her and Jane's return.

When Jane mentioned that she had met with Mr. Bingley and that he was planning to return to Netherfield within a day, Mrs. Bennet nearly swooned. "Oh, that is good news," she said. "I shall insist that your father call on him the moment he arrives and we will invite him for that family dinner as soon as possible."

Belatedly Mrs. Bennet remembered his presence as well. "And you, Mr. Darcy," she said coolly, "Do you intend to stay in Hertfordshire as well?"

"I shall stay as long as necessary."

Mrs. Bennet was confused. "As necessary for what, sir?"

"As long as necessary to speak with your husband, ma'am."

"Oh, you wish to speak with Mr. Bennet? You will find him in the library." She called for a servant, but then Elizabeth spoke. "Let me take Mr. Darcy to Papa," she offered.

Darcy followed Elizabeth out into the hallway.

"Do you wish to speak to your father first?" he asked quietly.

"I do, thank you," she said.

"Are you going to tell him to refuse my offer?"

Elizabeth's face flushed red. "I don't know. Everyone tells me that I have no choice."

He said, "Is there anything I can do to ease your mind?"

She said, "There are so many uncertainties. We are talking about a decision that will affect our entire lives." She smiled wryly. "Sometimes I think people take more care in choosing a Cook than in choosing a husband. At least with a Cook, one can taste a sauce before committing oneself."

Darcy's eyes widened and his breath caught. "You wish me to act as a husband with you?"

Now her face was red. "Oh no," she said quickly, but he saw that her gaze dropped to his lips for an instant before returning to his eyes.

Darcy felt like a fool. No wonder Elizabeth was skittish. He had never taken the time to woo her. He had merely expressed his desires and expected her to agree. And now she felt as if she was trapped by circumstances.

He lowered his voice. "Let me give you one kiss, then, for courage," he whispered.

She looked up at him bravely.

How he loved her. He cupped the side of her face with one hand and brought her lips closer to his. The first touch was brief and feather light. He pulled back to read her eyes. Yes? No?

She did not shrink back, so he kissed her again, firmer this time, longer and with one hand at the back of her waist.

"Mr. Darcy!"

Mr. Bennet's exclamation made him drop his hands and step back. "Sir," he said, mortified to have been caught kissing his daughter.

"Papa, we need to speak with you," Elizabeth said.

"Yes, I see that you do," Mr. Bennet said and glared at Darcy. "But you first, Elizabeth?"

"Yes, sir," she said and slipped into his study. Mr. Bennet closed the door in Darcy's face.

They spoke for nearly twenty minutes, their voices low and their conversation muffled through the heavy door. Darcy was tempted to bend down and listen through the keyhole, but he did not want to look more the fool, so he stood awkwardly, waiting.

Finally, Mr. Bennet opened the door. "Lizzy, go join your mother," he said briskly. "I shall speak with Mr. Darcy for some time."

Darcy stepped into the small study. It was a room with two comfortable leather chairs, walls covered with bookcases and a large desk in one corner by a window.

It was a larger room than Sir Lewis's retreat at Rosings, but Darcy supposed that it often served the same purpose.

Darcy stood and waited for his future father-in-law to speak.

"I don't like you, Mr. Darcy," Mr. Bennet said finally. "And I don't like the situation we are in."

"Neither do I, sir," Darcy said. "I would have much preferred to court your daughter in a more leisurely manner."

"Not too leisurely, Mr. Darcy," Mr. Bennet warned. "I don't want a repeat of what I observed in the hall before a minister pronounces you man and wife."

"Yes, sir."

"And Lizzy assures me that no liberties were taken while you were locked in together."

"That is correct."

Mr. Bennet nodded. "Very good. Now you may sit down and tell me how you intend to take care of my daughter."

ELIZABETH WAITED in the sitting room for Darcy to return. She relived the uncomfortable conversation with her father. He had made it clear that she had no choice but to marry Mr. Darcy unless she wanted to taint her entire family. "Fortunately, he is rich enough that you need not see him for weeks at a time, if you wish. He can live at one of his properties, while you live at another. But I would encourage you to find a way to tolerate him."

"I wish to do more than tolerate my husband."

"Sometimes that is the best that can be expected," Mr. Bennet said sadly. "But perhaps in time, when there are children, you will have more in common."

Elizabeth thought that was a generous thought, considering his own history.

"Thank you, sir."

While Darcy and her father spoke, Elizabeth also thought of their kisses in the hallway.

Darcy had been so careful, so sweet at first, and then the second kiss had ended too soon. She could not decide what she thought of that. She had never been kissed before, so she had no means for comparison, but she was surprised by how breathless she felt.

Eventually, Darcy returned to the sitting room with her father. Mr. Bennet made the announcement that Mr. Darcy had asked to marry Elizabeth and that he had given his permission.

Elizabeth looked at Mr. Darcy who looked grave. There was no turning back now, she thought miserably.

Mrs. Bennet's mouth gaped open with astonishment. "Mr. Darcy and Lizzy?" she repeated. "Truly? This is not one of your jokes, Mr. Bennet?"

"No, ma'am."

For a moment, Mrs. Bennet was so overcome that she could not speak, and when she did, it was near gibberish. "Oh, Mr. Darcy," she exclaimed. "The honour. Your fortune. I mean, it is such a pleasure. Good gracious! Oh, Lizzy, you dear girl."

Mr. Darcy spoke. "As much as I would enjoy spending more time with you –"

Liar, Elizabeth thought.

"I must go to London to acquire a license," Mr. Darcy continued.

"Oh yes," Mrs. Bennet said. "We would not delay you for a moment, sir."

Darcy took his leave, kissing Elizabeth's hand in farewell.

The minute he was gone, Mrs. Bennet said, "Oh Lizzy, just think of it. How rich and great you will be! A house in town! What pin money, what jewels, what carriages you will have! And such a charming man! So handsome, so tall!"

Mr. Bennet said loudly, "I will leave you to happiness, ma'am," and left to return to his study.

Lydia said, "Lizzy, how can you marry a man you hate?"

Mrs. Bennet laughed. "Don't be silly. No one hates ten thousand pounds a year."

CHAPTER THIRTEEN

Mrs. Bennet thought that nothing could make her happier than Elizabeth's engagement to Mr. Darcy, but she was wrong. For within another day, Mr. Bingley had returned to Netherfield and called on Mr. Bennet as well.

Elizabeth feared that the good news might give her mother apoplexy.

"Two daughters married!" Mrs. Bennet exclaimed. "Dearest Jane, I always knew how it would be. I was sure you could not be so beautiful for nothing! A double wedding. What will become of me? I shall go distracted! I am so happy. I am sure I sha'nt get a wink of sleep all night!"

The next week was a flurry of activity, with Mrs. Bennet making triumphant morning calls to all her friends and making wedding plans. Bingley was a daily visitor at Longbourn, coming frequently before breakfast and often remaining till after supper unless he had other invitations to dinner that he felt obliged to accept.

Elizabeth watched the ease of his conversation with her family and envied Jane her happiness.

Lydia thought all the fuss and excitement was excessive. She announced, "When I get married, I am going to elope to Gretna Green."

Mary looked up from a book of sermons to say, "That would not be proper."

"Oh pooh," Lydia said. "No one cares about that anymore."

Elizabeth smiled at her naivete. "Do you have someone in mind?"

"Not yet, but Wickham is free."

"I thought he was engaged to Miss King."

"No, for her uncle has taken her down to Liverpool, gone to stay."

Elizabeth thought that Miss King had made a fortunate escape.

Mrs. Bennet, overhearing their conversation said, "Oh Lydia, do not waste your time with Mr. Wickham. He is handsome in his redcoat, to be sure, but he doesn't have a feather to fly with. Look to Jane and Lizzy as your guide. Both of them are going to marry very wealthy men. I have no doubt that if you play your cards right, you could find a man twice as rich as Mr. Darcy and perhaps with a title as well."

Lydia's eyes sparkled with calculations. "I never thought of that."

"Mr. Darcy's uncle is an Earl," Mary said. "And according to Debrett's, his eldest son is unmarried."

"Is he a Viscount?" Mrs. Bennet asked.

Mary said, "He is."

Elizabeth was alarmed that her family knew more about Darcy's family than she did.

"See?" Mrs. Bennet said. "The possibilities are endless."

"Lizzy," Lydia pleaded. "When you're in London and married to Mr. Darcy, can I visit?"

"I know," Mrs. Bennet said excitedly. "You must go there for the Season. Ooh, just imagine being presented to the Queen!"

"I want to be presented, too!" Kitty said. "I have just as much right to go, for I am two years older!"

Elizabeth groaned, imagining Mr. Darcy's response. "I can make no promises," she said as Lydia danced about the room.

"When I am a Viscountess, I shall wear a diamond crown!"

Rather than missing her fiancé, Elizabeth began to fear his return, for if he spent too much time with her family, he would be tempted to leave her at the altar.

Mr. Darcy stayed away for two weeks, but he returned to stay at Netherfield. Servant gossip said he had brought his sister, Miss Darcy, and a carriage full of servants.

He called on Elizabeth the next morning.

How handsome he looked in his frock coat and buckskins. He was the picture of a landed gentleman, but he looked uncomfortable. "Miss Elizabeth," he said. "Would you care to walk with me outside?"

Mrs. Bennet laughed. "Feel free to spend as much time as you would like, Mr. Darcy! Don't hurry back, Lizzy."

Elizabeth, embarrassed, excused herself to fetch a bonnet and a shawl.

Within a few minutes, they were walking outside in the wilderness garden to the side of her house.

Elizabeth watched his serious expression and thought, *He has changed his mind. All of my arguments have convinced him that he does not want to marry me after all.* But for some reason, the thought did not please her. Was she starting to care for him?

He said, "I have thought for days about your comment that people spend more effort choosing a servant than choosing a spouse. And to some extent, I think you are correct. At least servants come with verbal recommendations or written characters."

Elizabeth nodded. "That is true. Our most recent lady's maid was recommended by Mrs. Wyatt in Meryton."

He smiled wryly, "Unfortunately, I do not have a prior wife who can attest to my excellence as a husband."

Elizabeth smiled. "That would be its own problem."

"Indeed. I would not want to go to jail for bigamy." They walked together in silence for a minute and he said, "But I do have some character references."

"Mr. Bingley speaks very highly of you."

Darcy said, "Yes, and I have more."

Elizabeth looked at him closely, amused. "Are you saying you have letters?"

"No, I have brought people for you to interview. Some of them are my servants, and you may think they are biased in my favour, but I have charged them to tell you the truth, warts and all."

She was touched by his efforts to please her, but she said lightly, "Do you have warts, Mr. Darcy?"

"I am not a perfect man," he said seriously. "But I hope I am a good one."

At that moment, Elizabeth realized that perhaps she could love him, after all. She said, "I will speak to your people, but where? I don't think it wise to do it where my mother can see it."

"I agree. Would you care to walk with me now to Netherfield?"

"I would like that, yes. And as my mother said, we are to take all the time we want."

Darcy offered her his arm, which she took gladly. "I am beginning to like your mother," he said.

Elizabeth laughed.

At Netherfield, Darcy arranged for her to be in a sitting room where she could interview each of his references privately. Mr. Bingley was the first. "I don't exactly know why I am here," he began as he sat across from her. "But Darcy says you want to ask me some questions about him?"

Elizabeth said, "Yes, thank you. Darcy wants me to know more about him before we tie the knot."

"What do you want to know?"

"How did you meet?"

"At school, but I did not know him well for he was three years older. Then later, one day at Tattersalls, I was going to bid on a horse and I saw him watching me. I raised one eyebrow as if asking his opinion and he shook his head slightly, so I did not buy it. We spoke outside later, dined together, and we have been friends ever since."

"What do you think is his best quality?"

"Loyalty," Bingley said. "I would trust him with my life."

This was praise indeed, and Elizabeth supposed that even when Darcy had kept Bingley from Jane, he meant it for the best. "Is there anything you would change about him, if you could?"

"At times I thought he was too formal, too rigid in his thinking, but his love for you has changed him. He is more relaxed now."

Had his love for her changed him? Elizabeth thought she saw some changes herself. He was polite to her family and he smiled more often. "Thank you," she said.

The next person she spoke with was Mrs.

Reynolds, the housekeeper of Pemberley. She was a respectable-looking, elderly woman, much less fine and more civil than Elizabeth would have expected. Mrs. Reynolds said, "Mr. Darcy is the best landlord, and the best master that ever lived. There is not one of his tenants or servants but what will give him a good name. He follows in the footsteps of his father, God rest his soul, who was a most excellent man, fair in all his dealings and affable to the poor."

"How long have you worked at Pemberley?"

"Nearly twenty-five years, ma'am. I came to Pemberley when Mr. Darcy was four years old."

Elizabeth smiled. "What was he like as a child?"

"He was the sweetest tempered, most generous hearted boy in the world."

This surprised her. "Did he ever cause trouble?"

"Not really, except when he was with George Wickham, the steward's son. But over the years, they went their separate ways. I understand that Mr. Wickham has gone into the army and turned out very wild."

"So I've heard," Elizabeth said.

"There has been none of that from Mr. Darcy. He takes his duties as Master of Pemberley and as guardian to his sister seriously.

Elizabeth assumed that he would take his duties

as her husband seriously as well. She thought of the effort it took for him to arrange these interviews.

Mrs. Reynolds added, "Some people call him proud, but I am sure I never say anything of it. To my fancy, it is only because he does not rattle away like other young men."

Elizabeth smiled. Darcy definitely did not rattle away. There was something to be said about a man who chose his words wisely and meant what he said. She might not always like what Darcy said, but she knew he was honest.

After Mrs. Reynolds, Elizabeth spoke to Mr. Bowles, his valet, whom she had met earlier. At her inquiry, he admitted that Mr. Darcy did have a temper and was known to swear on occasion. "But only upon the greatest provocation," he assured her. I don't believe I've heard him swear more than five times within as many years." He also told her that Mr. Darcy liked his home to be orderly. "He doesn't like surprises, ma'am."

That was good to know, Elizabeth thought.

After Mr. Bowles, came Mr. Spencer, Darcy's steward, a wiry, grey-haired man in his fifties. He came into the room with several leather-bound account books, ready to share Mr. Darcy's financial secrets. Elizabeth was astounded. She did not know if even Mr. Gardiner shared all his financial information with Mrs. Gardiner. "I don't need all the details," she told that earnest gentleman. "But you can give me a summary."

Mr. Spencer told her of the Pemberley properties, the Town House, a hunting box in Leicestershire, and another estate in Scotland. In addition, Darcy owned part of two canals and had inherited an interest in several mines in Cornwall.

"Is he a frugal man?" Elizabeth asked.

"He's not a miser," Mr. Spencer said. "And he's not one to quibble over a shilling here or there, but he is careful. He does not borrow money and he's no gambler. In all my years, I have never seen him make payments on gambling debts or for expensive ladybirds, either."

"Good heavens," Elizabeth said, embarrassed by this frank disclosure.

Mr. Spencer looked her straight in the eyes. "Pardon me, miss, but if my daughter was getting married, that is one of the things I would want to know. Many a young man has ruined his fortunes and brought home diseases to wife after spending time with harlots."

"Yes, thank you," Elizabeth said. She realized

that this was one topic her father would not have thought to discuss with Mr. Darcy.

After Mr. Spencer, Miss Darcy came to speak with her. "Miss Bennet," Miss Darcy said. "I am so glad to see you again."

"Call me Elizabeth, please."

"And you must call me Georgiana."

Elizabeth nodded. "I will."

Georgiana said, "William says I am to answer all your questions truthfully."

Elizabeth smiled. "You call him William, not Fitzwilliam?"

"No, for when I was younger Fitzwilliam was too long a name."

Elizabeth smiled, wondering what she would call him when they were married. In her mind, he had been Mr. Darcy for so long that even 'Darcy' seemed like a presumption. She said, "Tell me about your parents."

"My mother was very kind. She liked to play the pianoforte and sing. When I was young, we often played in the gardens at Pemberley. She designed a rose garden. She died when I was six."

"And your father?"

"He died when I was ten."

"And since then, your brother has been your guardian."

"Yes."

"Is he a stern taskmaster?"

Georgiana said, "No, not at all. If anything, he has been too lenient. He is forever buying something to make me happy."

"Are you often together at Pemberley?"

"For most of the summer, usually."

Except for last summer when Georgiana went to Ramsgate, but Elizabeth would not refer to that.

"And in the winter months, when I am at school, he is often in Town and visits me."

"Do you like school?" Elizabeth asked.

"I like learning," Georgiana said carefully. "But I would prefer to learn at home."

"That is how I learnt," Elizabeth said. "But I know there are gaps in my education."

"My brother says you are very well read," Georgiana said quickly.

"Your brother is too kind."

Georgiana said, "I am hoping that once you are wed that I can leave school and come home."

Elizabeth said, "I would enjoy that, but that decision will be your brother's."

Georgiana nodded. "I know and Mrs. Annesley,

she's my companion, she says that you and William may wish to spend more time together alone once you are wed."

Darcy had never mentioned a honeymoon or wedding trip, so Elizabeth did not know what he would prefer. She asked, "Do you consider your brother to be a kind man?"

"I do," Georgiana said. "He was very kind last summer, when I made a very big mistake. I know he told you about Mr. Wickham. How I almost ran away with him."

Elizabeth reached across to touch her hand kindly. "You don't have to tell me if you don't wish to."

"No. It is good to talk about it. There really hasn't been anyone to tell. Except for William, and it just makes him angry."

"At you?"

"Oh, no. At Wickham. William has never been mad at me. He says he should have warned me about Wickham and done a better job of protecting me."

"I have met Mr. Wickham," Elizabeth said. "He can be very charming."

"Yes, but I should have known that he was not honourable when he wanted to elope."

Elizabeth remembered Darcy saying that an elopement with her would be easier, but in the end, he did as she wished, speaking first to her uncle and then to her father, honouring their wishes.

Georgiana added, "William says that the right man will ask his permission."

It was obvious to Elizabeth that Georgiana trusted and idolized her brother. Nearly half of her sentences began with "William says." Elizabeth asked one more question. "Does he listen to you?"

Georgiana hesitated, then said, "Most of the time. But sometimes I sense that he is thinking of something else and not paying attention to me."

Elizabeth smiled. Georgiana was honest to a fault. "I think that is true of almost all men," Elizabeth said. "Even excellent men like your brother."

CHAPTER FOURTEEN

Darcy paced the floor as Georgiana spoke with Elizabeth. What was taking them so long? What were they talking about? He heard them laugh together and he began to think it was a mistake to bring people for Elizabeth to interrogate.

Finally, Georgiana stepped out of the drawing room.

"Well?" he demanded.

Georgiana smiled. "I think she likes you, William."

Darcy felt his heart lighten.

"And she wishes to speak to you."

Darcy burst through the drawing room doors. "Elizabeth," he said as he approached her. "What is your verdict?"

She rose to her feet and smiled at him. "I cannot decide whether you are incredibly brave or foolish."

He tried to read her expression. "In what way?"

She walked up to him and touched the side of his face with a tender caress. "You are either very brave for letting others share your secrets or very foolish for trusting me to keep them."

He was thrilled by her words. He turned his head to kiss her hand. "Dearest Elizabeth," he said.

Her eyes shone with love. "Dearest William."

NEARLY ALL OF Meryton came to see the two eldest Bennet daughters marry their wealthy suitors. Some people whispered that Darcy had locked Elizabeth in a dungeon until she agreed to marry him, but others noticed the way the two smiled at each other as they spoke their vows and dismissed the gossip as unfounded.

Mr. Bennet joked that having two daughters marry on one day was a great economy and that he planned to have the remaining three marry next, if he could line up suitors.

Lydia pouted when she heard this and

exclaimed, "I shall never marry if I have to wait for Mary to secure a beau!"

At the wedding breakfast, Darcy cornered Colonel Fitzwilliam who had ridden into Meryton in the middle of the night, just in time to attend the wedding. "Tell me about Anne," Darcy said.

"Well, she is married right and tight, now," the Colonel said. "I was one of the witnesses at the anvil."

Darcy nodded. "So she is Signora Bianchi now. Do you think she will be happy?"

The Colonel said, "I think so. She did not feel well from all the travelling and Bianchi was attentive." The Colonel smiled. "I ate supper with Bianchi while she was resting and we talked for hours. I was surprised to learn that unlike Wickham, the elopement was not his idea. Anne came up with the plans herself, and she was the one who proposed to him. She was quite insistent."

"Like mother like daughter?" Darcy said, thinking of that locked door. He supposed he would never know if Lady Catherine had planned it or if it had happened by chance.

"Bianchi seemed appreciative."

"Very good," Darcy said. He hoped that Anne would live long enough to enjoy her foreign lover.

He looked across the room at Elizabeth who was radiant in her wedding finery – a pale green dress with gold lace. He watched as she spoke with Sir William Lucas, accepting his well-wishes.

But then, as if aware of his gaze, she turned and smiled at him with her fine eyes and Darcy felt his heart flood with love. Despite all his flaws, he was the luckiest man in England, for Elizabeth Bennet loved him.

EPILOGUE

MEET me in the wine cellar.

Elizabeth glanced at the note left on her writing desk. She smiled, closed her day book, and calmly walked past the library and Gallery, then downstairs and through the kitchen. Mrs. Reynolds called out, "Mrs. Darcy, do you need anything?"

"No, thank you," Elizabeth said pleasantly. "I am merely going to choose a wine for dinner."

"Yes, ma'am."

Elizabeth opened the door to the wine cellar and stepped into the cool dark air. She lit one of the candles that was on a shelf on the wall and carried it with her.

After another set of stairs, she came to a room – not as large as the cellar at Rosings, but with a table and several chairs. Adjoining rooms contained shelves of wine. The room was lit by a standing candelabra, making light flicker on the walls and ceiling. She set her candle down and started to explore.

She turned a corner and suddenly a man was before her. Without saying a word, he kissed her fiercely and pushed her back against the cold stone walls.

Elizabeth sighed with satisfaction, letting him press against her without struggle or protest. She wove her fingers into his thick dark hair to draw him closer.

Eventually he pulled back. "Do you know what day it is?" he whispered and then kissed her throat.

She shivered at the familiar thrill. "Guessing from that kiss, it is our second anniversary." The anniversary of their night in Rosing's wine cellar, not their second wedding anniversary.

He continued down her neck. "Precisely. And today I can do what I only dreamed of doing back then."

Elizabeth smiled. So much had changed since then. "If I had known what you were thinking, I would not have been so calm."

"Especially since you still hated me."

"Not for long," she argued. "By midnight, you were beginning to change my mind."

"Perhaps I should write a letter thanking Anne."

"No, don't. I don't think you should encourage her. Even though our story ended well, I don't think it wise to dose people with laudanum."

He smiled down at her. "You are right of course, as you almost always are." He kissed her once more for good measure, then took her hand and guided her back to the table where Elizabeth now noticed that there was a bottle of champagne and a plate of fruit and bread and cheese waiting for them.

Much better than Lady Catherine's meat pies, Elizabeth thought as she sat down. She nibbled a piece of bread with cheese and watched as her husband of nearly two years uncorked the bottle. How tall and strong he looked in his shirt sleeves and waistcoat. He often removed his coat when they were alone, since he had learned to enjoy a more casual attire.

He poured the sparkling wine into two glasses and asked her. "To what shall we toast?" he asked. One lock of his dark hair hung down on his fore-head, making her fingers itch to push it back. He wore his hair slightly longer now, another one of her suggestions.

But he had changed her style as well. She only wore a corset on her most formal occasions because he said he preferred to feel wife rather than whalebone when he put his arm around her.

"To Jane," she suggested and they both took a sip of champagne.

"Is she sleeping now?" Darcy asked.

"Yes, thankfully." Their beautiful daughter, six months old now, had been awake most of the night. Her nurse thought she was teething and recommended rubbing her gums with a cold spoon.

Elizabeth had already written to Jane for her advice. Jane's son was several month's older. The Bingley's had moved closer to Pemberley a year ago and the two families visited often. Elizabeth had gone to Jane's lying in and she had come to hers. Their friend Charlotte had not been so fortunate. She had died two weeks after giving birth. Mr. Collins, grief stricken and seeking a mother for his son, had turned his eyes towards Longbourn a second time. Mary accepted his proposal gratefully. She seemed happy to take charge of the Parsonage and had even given some advice to Lady Catherine on occasion.

Lady Catherine had changed as well. Anne did not have a baby, yet, but Signor Bianchi had invited most of his family to live with them at Rosings - his widowed mother, three unmarried sisters and a drunken ne'er do well cousin who seduced Mrs. Jenkinson.

Rosings Park was now quite lively and Lady Catherine had no need for Darcy and the Colonel to visit to provide entertainment.

Lydia had recently become Viscountess, as she had planned, although her husband was not Darcy's cousin. She enjoyed taking precedence over her sisters. She drove a light blue curricle all about Town and hosted extravagant parties that included many officers. There were wagers in White's that the Viscount, aged seventy-eight, would not last a year.

Surprisingly, Kitty was still at home. She had enjoyed a Season in London, but now preferred to stay at Longbourn. When she visited Pemberley, she spent hours in the stables. "I don't know what to do for her," Elizabeth had said and Darcy told her not to fret.

"She is still young. She will find her own way," he said, just as Georgiana was finding her own way.

Recently Georgiana had talked about starting her own school.

"What are you thinking?" Darcy asked.

Elizabeth smiled at him. "Sorry," she murmured. "I was lost in thought. Thinking how much has changed in the past two years."

He sipped his champagne and nodded. "One thing hasn't changed, though."

She recognized the warm tone of his voice. "And what is that?"

"My love for you."

For a moment, Elizabeth basked in his approval. She knew the greatest changes had been in her own life. She had gone from being an independent, slightly cynical young woman to being Mistress of Pemberley, happily married wife and mother. She thanked Providence for the miracle of her life. She rose to her feet and raised her glass. "I have another toast," she said.

Darcy watched her, his eyes smiling at her. "What is that?"

"To locked doors!"

The End

AUTHOR'S NOTE:

I hope you enjoyed *All Night with Mr. Darcy*. I have often joked that my favorite stories are about two angry people locked in a room until they resolve their differences. I also believe that Darcy and Elizabeth are two intelligent, honest people who fall in love with each other as they talk. The proposal at Hunsford is the first time they truly begin to understand each other. Then Darcy's letter is his chance to explain himself further. Elizabeth gets to read and reread that letter for months and over time, her feelings change. I've always wondered what would happen if Darcy and Elizabeth did not have that separation between the First Proposal and Meeting Again at Pemberley – what if they were forced by circumstances to deal with each other? This story is my answer to that question.

I also liked creating a new version of Anne de Bourgh. Since she does not say anything in the original text, I often wonder what she is thinking.

Ah, the joy of writing Pride and Prejudice Variations. I get to change circumstances and see what happens.

Happy reading,

Jane Grix

Manufactured by Amazon.ca
Bolton, ON

43826001R00099